FROM DESPAIR
TO WHERE

FROM DESPAIR TO WHERE

Lee Geraint Ingman

First paperback edition 2022

ISBNs:
Paperback: 978-1-80227-685-5
ebook: 978-1-80227-686-2

Contents

Part Two

Part Three

Prologue

Michael stood on the doorstep of the now empty Victorian house. The sign above him read "sold" but he decided to let himself in.

Standing at the threshold, he made use of a spare key which he had kept in reserve for this particular jaunt and, whilst unlocking the door, he found himself lost in an attempt to dispel the bad memories which his former home always elicited.

All through his life he'd hoped and prayed for some sort of closure from this particular brand of torment. So far though, his memories stood firm, providing him with nothing but an assortment of negativities. The old house persisted to haunt him on so many different levels.

Silence greeted him as he crossed over the threshold. From the damp smelling hallway, he made his way upstairs and across the landing to the door belonging to the household's one and only bathroom. Sunlight glistened off every surface; he was glad to see the cleaner he hired had done a good job. But after he sat himself on the lid of the toilet seat, his gaze turned to the floor and, for a while, he found it hard not to imagine its surface stained the darkest shade of crimson.

He sat there, thinking. A thirty-eight-year-old man considering his past and his present as the cold water tap dripped incessantly into the room's wide free-standing bathtub.

After a while, he stood.

His mind continued on its reverie as his feet took him out of the bathroom and into the room which his parents had once shared. The view from out of the window was picturesque, comprising a few abandoned barns, a shallow river and a rolling Welsh valley. A scattering of hills also dominated the horizon, all situated within this north-eastern slice of Gwynedd.

However, the air was both damp and chilly and he shivered as he breathed it in. Feeling both cold and miserable, he left the upper floor and made his way along the downstairs corridor to a cellar whose ancient lock lay broken and discarded on the hallway floor. He'd used a crowbar to wrench it free last week when thoughts of his own past had led him here. Now, as then, he pushed open the door and began to descend the steps into the murky interior. The cellar itself was claustrophobic yet he soon found himself crouching down in a corner.

Too many memories assaulted him. So much so that, this morning whilst his father was being laid to his "eternal rest", Michael had chosen to come here to confront whatever demons his dad's callous and corrosive persona had instilled in him. *It's hard to be a good person*, he surmised, *when you find yourself dragging all this weight around with you.*

However, his life had become much more tolerable since his childhood exposure to his father's abuse, neglect and extreme violence had been halted by his sudden departure some twenty years previously. Michael had taken sole possession and had inhabited the property alone for the past decade or so but forgetting all the darker memories he'd inherited along with the bricks and mortar now had to be his top priority. His state of being in the present would have to be confronted with the same degree of attention as the potential of his future.

Selling up had been a good first step because, just recently, within the walls and beneath the roofline of this property, too many reminders of his father's madness had started to invade both his mind and soul.

Michael began to cry uncontrollably.

How long he stayed that way he couldn't know for sure without a wristwatch, but he guessed it to be around midday as the church bells had begun to chime, calling forwards in this instance, all who cared to pay their final respects to another departed but morally dubious soul. His father's.

It should have been a good time to look to the future, but the past still held him in its grip. As he left the cellar and exited the house, locking the front door behind him for the very last time, he posted his one remaining key through the letterbox in a small and final attempt at letting it all go. But letting go would soon become his top priority as he had already planned to say his goodbyes to these memories in his own particular way.

PART ONE

One

The town, which had served as an unforgiving home for him since early childhood, stood on the border at the western edge of Wales. A landscape marred by hundreds of years of violent conflict between both the Welsh and the English. The latter unwelcome landlords for many passing centuries.

In the present, the fact was that for many of those who walked its narrow streets and lived within its age-old terraced cottages the town was now just a place to spend their diminishing years and rest their heads at night. Many had relocated from the cities to invest their pensions on the peace and quiet of the place, but it still had its exceptions.

As he made his way to the old derelict schoolhouse, Michael checked his wristwatch as well as his pace. It was now two in the morning and his breathing had grown fierce. He inhaled the smoke from his thirty-fourth cigarette of the past twenty-four hours. The nicotine did little to curb the anxiety which had served as an unwelcome guest ever since the days of his own blighted youth.

Emotion was a major stumbling block for him. Thoughts and feelings connected with his current state and his past, reminded him of long ago and soon merged with the depressing thoughts of his present. What he needed now was some form of panacea. Suddenly, he found he had made his way to within the last few yards of his goal.

Glancing over his shoulder, Michael momentarily redirected his gaze from the looming expanse of concrete and stone ahead and surveyed the rest of the town to his rear, but he could see very little. Everything was either swamped in a deep lightless black or silhouetted in sodium streetlight orange, adding to the mystique of this place and providing him with an early morning snapshot of its deserted streets.

In front of him stood a harsh right-angle of crafted stonework and heavy brickwork shouldering a worn and unpaved pathway. He knew from memory that this path encircled the entire building, conveniently providing a shortcut straight through this long-abandoned structure. Weeds grew at its edges and the once well-trodden trail was discernible now only by the sparse spacing of the flora growing along its surface.

As he strolled through the rectangle of yard separating the indoor reception areas from the classrooms, memories of his past colluded and conspired to instigate a pivotal course of action.

Can you hate a building? he thought as he walked.

The place had stood silent for a good couple of decades now. However, it had also been within eyesight of his former home ever since its construction. Therefore, it had remained an unpleasant reminder of those brutal and tumultuous times each and every time he had glanced out of his bedroom window. However, Michael had already concluded he didn't specifically hate the old, neglected schoolhouse. Instead, he hated the memories which were unwaveringly triggered by just the sight of the place. These were, for him, the ultimate source of his choking, unexpressed rage. Memories which had held him back from the real world with its abundance of possibilities of which he had very rarely taken any advantage of.

Maybe what he was about to do was in some small way an attempt to eradicate such memories in a similar attempt to look to the future or was he just a sad and bitter person out to symbolically settle a score?

True, he had been hurt. However, was he actually entitled to channel his rage outwardly into some sort of symbolic attempt at eradicating his own internal demons? Demons which were invariably instigated by both the memories and emotions which he had kept stored away in the back of his mind for the best part of a quarter of a century.

Getting back to reality, Michael found himself fidgeting with an old and rusty key as he walked. In the near distance, the incessant silence and seemingly limitless depths of the overgrown playground became nothing more than a passing curiosity as he directed his attention away from its loosely defined borders.

A chill ran down his spine as he strode on; his attention divided between the effort to maintain the constant rhythm required to walk and the need to keep a close watch for any signs of trespass. Nothing was damaged though. The windows and doors looked as solid and strong as when they were first nailed shut. There was a little graffiti, but this was nothing new. He knew it all like the back of his hand. Immature scribbles, carvings or flecks of spray paint thrown lopsidedly off-centre by some inexperienced scribe. Modern art held its roots in expressions such as these but there was nothing imaginative or endearing in any of the ill-conceived declarations scattered along the walls of this dark, secluded side of the building. Discarded and rusting lager cans, empty wine or cider bottles and the occasional cigarette butt or cannabis roach, lay in an intermittent line along the pathway.

Ahead of him, a rectangle of stone-encased darkness provided a relief from the starkness of the view and Michael headed straight towards this door; the greasy key still in his palm.

At the school's main entrance, the rusty key fitted smartly into its cradle and with a swift and precise flick of his wrist, Michael soon had the bolt free of its lock. He watched with glee as the door swung halfway inwards without the need for a nudge from either his shoulder or his hand. Simultaneously, he felt the wave of depression lift as he crossed below the dilapidated doorway's wooden arch, soon seeing how a quarter-century's worth of weathering and neglect had caused as much damage to the building's interior as it had to its exterior.

The rest of the structure had suffered the same fate and Michael soon discovered that its increasingly sorry state served to lift him slightly out of his transient, unexpected mood. Before proceeding though, he scanned the outside field for any kind of movement and, only when he was fully satisfied with the view, did he step forwards and push the door closed. Securing the bolt behind him, his torch illuminated the main corridor with an ambient multi-angled brightness.

A faint smell of petroleum emanated from a single flight of steps leading down to a cellar of damp stonework, loose mortar and cracked tiling. By rights, he should not have been able to snatch even a whiff of the stuff, but he had been clumsy the last time he had been here, carelessly spilling petrol onto the floor where it had dried and evaporated.

He wasn't heading that way though. Everything that could have been done down there had been done and that was almost true for the rest of the place too. *Almost*, he thought, *but not quite.*

This would be his final visit, and his last opportunity to visit. All that was needed was a single spark produced at the right moment and in the right place. Nestled in the inside pocket of his slightly worn leather jacket was a second-hand Zippo lighter.

It was difficult to rig the average butane lighter to hold a flame for any extended period and so he had bought the Zippo at a car boot sale the previous week. However, he hadn't bothered to buy spare flints or a supply of extra lighter fluid for it because this lighter would only see the light of day again when all the dust, debris and rubble was cleared away. The land might be useful to developers, so maybe he'd be doing quite a few people quite a few favours.

Losing this thought, he crossed the room and passed by the cellar entrance. Another doorway opened onto a narrow walkway and soon it was only the soft echoes of his footsteps and a mounting sense of unease accompanying him.

His reflection, a distorted and insubstantial doppelgänger, stared back at him from a dust-coated window as Michael flicked the beam of his torch directly ahead of him. Soon, the apparition was replaced with the view of an untended garden. Michael knew this area had once served as an outdoor dining area reserved for members of staff, and as a showpiece for visiting guests. Now the benches were rotten, the flowerbeds overwhelmed by weeds and the centrepiece water fountain at its heart stood both lifeless and neglected.

Back inside, nothing stirred. The halls were unnaturally silent with not even the usual creaks and squeaks of a building settling in on itself. Could it be that the silence of this moment would shape the course of things to come?

Should he move backwards, he could easily return to the dull, predictable lifestyle which he'd chosen to adopt during the past decade. A sideways move, meanwhile, might entail surrendering his fate to the inescapable scars of his own past and, quite possibly, leave him wide open to a descent into some form of madness.

With a sigh, Michael retrieved the Zippo from his inside pocket and headed left. The hollow echo of his footsteps followed as he walked, breaking the silence as decades-old dust was shifted under his feet. Up ahead of him, the floor angled slowly upwards towards a small gymnasium where a gallon and a half of petroleum lay in the shadows.

His Zippo gave a dull click as he forced the lid open to reveal its wick, flint and striking wheel. Within moments, the flame was glowing fiercely. He let the lighter fall to Earth as he continued his ascent to the gym, breathing in the stuffy air as his heart beat harder and more frantically. Fear and trepidation had been regular companions whenever he had made his way beneath the canopy of this familiar roofline. Although his memories were decades old, the pain and despair of his school days reminded him of both the physical and mental scars which he still carried with him from those dark, tumultuous times.

Seconds passed as he stood in the gym doorway. Up ahead of him, equipment which hadn't been sold or transferred to another school stood in a chaotic heap beneath the towering expanse of the tall and silent climbing frames standing against an eastern- facing wall.

Pausing for a moment, he allowed deeper memories to play with his senses. Then, in a rising, seething rage, he picked up the petrol can and sent it crashing down the sloping corridor to meet with his Zippo.

In moments, the hallway erupted in a gush of flames and Michael wasted no time in exiting the building via a fire escape door. He sprinted for the safety of the playing fields as the fire took hold. Soon, the entire basement level was engulfed in a torrent of flames whose insatiable hunger would eventually consume the roof supports and send its slates sailing through the night's sky.

Minutes passed as he watched. Eventually, the sound of sirens pierced the clear air and Michael's breathing grew fierce, but the wail of the emergency vehicles was swiftly cancelled out by a deep feeling of elation. However, when he finally wiped at his streaming eyes, he wondered whether his actions had been sparked by revenge or as some symbolic attempt to gain a certain kind of reparation. Or could this be just the beginning of his descent into insanity?

Two

Two short days later, Michael found himself driving with a hangover. It was a bastard. *However, at least I'm on a bypass,* he thought. On a meandering country B-road, he would probably have wrapped his car around the nearest tree by now. He regretted having plied himself with booze at a Travelodge and its adjacent bar the previous night, but he supposed it was just part of the release he was now seeking in his life. Thankfully, this bypass was relatively straight, at least when compared with the other twisting, turning lanes that crisscrossed the Welsh countryside.

Although he still had a considerable way to go, he intended to stop at the next service station for some strong coffee and something to line his stomach. Soon, a sign on the left helpfully told him the nearest stop-off point was just five miles away, so he'd probably reach it in as many minutes. That gave him time to ponder things for a short while.

He'd sold his house and everything in it just a few days ago and, following his father's funeral, was currently looking for pastures new. Where that would be, he didn't yet know. He'd spend the night in another Travelodge or bed and breakfast, and then tomorrow morning he'd keep driving until an opportunity presented itself. After all, he had money in the bank, no ties — whether family, social or otherwise — and was also still young enough to start again. There was still time to begin the process of forgetting, and — he hoped — leaving his past in the past.

At the age of thirty-eight, he remained single and childless. Given his present situation, the absence of priorities and commitments such as partnership and parenthood were a blessing in disguise; these factors would only have entrenched him down in everyday life anyway. However, Michael had acquired the capacity to switch off from the familiar and mundane — a gift completely welcomed by him. Thanks to his extremely fertile imaginary world, he'd developed the capacity to counter the more depressing elements of his gloomy past.

He still had aspirations but as he headed towards middle age, the negative experiences of his younger self had undermined his confidence and his dreams, resulting in a jaded view of life. Still, for a man in his late thirties he wasn't doing too badly. He'd been drug-free — if not alcohol-free — for ten years and he'd found, for the better part of this decade, clean-living had transformed itself into clean-thinking. He had started to enjoy pondering and even philosophising on life. On the other hand, he had become increasingly averse to sharing his thoughts with others.

Michael would happily converse in bars with the temporary drinking buddies he met, but he would never share anything personal or express his own philosophical point of view. His mind was locked to strangers, almost like some living library or art exhibition open only to himself. Discussing anything from the serious to the trite with his mother had always had a soothing and therapeutic effect on him during his childhood and adolescence. Since then, and particularly throughout the past decade or so, he'd settled for the pretension and feigned concern of strangers.

He shook off all such thoughts as he found himself nearing the rest area on the outskirts of yet another town. He was hungry and mentally weary. He brought his car to a halt in the carpark of the Little Chef restaurant, turned off the ignition and made for the entrance.

Having taken a corner table, he looked through the window and out across the carpark while he waited for the waitress. It was empty apart from a few HGVs and a family car. His own vehicle, a sporty, black Toyota Celica, looked completely out of place. It had cost him a small fortune, but he hadn't minded. He had inherited a fair amount of money both from his mother ten years previously and, more recently, his father. This soon-to-be-inherited, guilt-ridden contribution would provide a significant boost to his already substantial bank balance.

Up to receiving his mother's inheritance, he had worked only in menial jobs offering minimum wage, mainly in the service industry or shelf-stacking in local supermarkets and shops. His favourite though, had been the night work at various factories and warehouses on the outskirts of his nearest town. The night work tended to be less hectic with management more focused on organising the day shifts. He found things were much more quiet and far less regimented, and he had loved the satisfaction of crawling into bed every Monday morning just as most other people were starting their five-a-week day shifts.

Michael would stay up for a few hours after finishing his shift work at seven and, in the spring and summer, would enjoy watching the world rouse. When the sun began to appear over the horizon, calling most of the population out of their beds, he'd be content to sleep most of his day away. On the few days he had free during his forty-eight-hour working week, he'd find himself either calling the employment agency for extra shifts or wandering aimlessly around the house he had then shared with his mother. Most of the time, she'd be working on his days off and he'd often feel lost at the prospect of filling up the hours while he waited for her to return from her day job.

Back then, his life had been lacking any kind of social structure and most of the time, he'd retreat into his own imaginary world. Unfortunately, he increasingly found it a depressing place.

He tried to break free of such thoughts and turned his gaze to the menu, but he could already feel a black mood descending.

The restaurant's only other customer was sitting across the aisle, four tables away. She had blonde hair, though Michael was unsure if it was her natural colour, and she was currently gazing out towards the carpark, the exit and the bypass beyond it. She looked pretty in the sunlight, but pretty women were hardly ever alone so he returned his attention to the menu until the waitress arrived, notebook in hand, to take his order.

Michael took off his jacket, folded his arms, and waited.

During his meal, he found himself glancing over at the blonde woman, waiting for her boyfriend or companion to appear, but no one arrived to join her. He wondered whether she, like Michael himself on any other day, would be far too lost in her own thoughts to notice the rather pathetic-looking figure sitting just a few tables away. As he ate, he began to sense his own desperate need for contact. Even just a quick glance in his direction would be enough. But then suddenly he got his wish as, just as he was finishing his dessert, she caught his eye.

She paid her bill and walked towards his table.

"That yours?" she asked, indicating his car.

Despite having a mouthful of food and feeling awkward, he nodded.

"Got a smoke?"

Swallowing, he passed her the pack, then said, "Keep them."

"Thanks," she said and walked outside.

He looked over his shoulder and noticed her lighting up whilst still staying close to the entrance. Was she waiting for someone?

With his initial wish for contact fulfilled, he justified his failure to attempt to expand the interaction further. He was sure he would have become tongue-tied if their brief exchange had progressed into a full-blown conversation. He always found that beyond the usual, banal pleasantries, he had nothing much else to say to anybody, at least when he was sober. And so, he drained the last of his coffee, paid his bill and headed towards the door. She was still there. Having finished her cigarette, she was gazing out across the carpark, her expression empty. He passed her by, but turned back when she spoke.

"Where you headed?" she asked.

He thought for a while, then said, "East."

She smiled. "Same here. Any chance of a lift?"

After considering for a second or two, he nodded and then walked towards his car with the blonde woman in tow. He meant to ask her name but decided that ultimately it was unimportant. Whatever her name, she was now along for the ride — wherever it might take them.

After making herself comfortable in the passenger seat, she pulled out the half-packet of cigarettes he'd given her earlier and offered him one before lighting up herself and winding down the window. Michael did the same but neglected to open his own window as he hated the sound of the wind and the way it battered his ears and tousled his hair. He switched on the engine and put the car into gear.

They had a clear run of all three lanes on the bypass and he took the inner one, driving a pinch too fast and gunning the engine, enjoying the speed. He liked to live a little dangerously and, he surmised, most men in possession of a fast car would find themselves taking full advantage of the added horsepower.

For a while, he forgot about his passenger. If she had been alarmed at the speed of their departure, she certainly hadn't shown it.

When she tossed her cigarette stub out of the window, Michael glimpsed the track marks peppering her left forearm.

She caught his gaze and quickly pulled down her sleeve.

Insulin or heroin? he wondered, but soon shrugged off the thought. Right now, he had far too much on his mind and, even if his suspicions were right, was she really likely to admit her addiction to a man she had just met? Obviously, drugs were bad news. Capable of delivering bouts of all-encompassing pleasure but also, during the inevitable comedown, providing a person with a hindsight that invited deep feelings of guilt and regret. And, likely as not, empty pockets.

Deciding on a dose of silence, Michael and his new companion drove; the woman staring blankly out of the window whilst lighting cigarette after cigarette.

Michael wondered if her state-of-mind might be as chaotic as his own. Misery loves company, his mother used to tell him. She had been full of old-fashioned anecdotes and philosophies. At that moment, he missed her intensely. Realising he craved that comfort and empathy, he decided to break the silence.

"What's your name?" he asked.

She turned towards him. "Lisa."

"Michael."

She smiled. "Hello Michael."

"How far east are you going?"

"The next town." She paused. "Just out for a drive?"

He shook his head. "Not exactly. I've become what you might call a drifter."

"A drifter in a sports car?"

"Pretty much," he replied. Then, after a pause, he added, "An inheritance brought it my way."

She frowned. "From your parents?"

"From both of them. As of a week or so ago."

"I'm sorry."

Michael considered for a moment, then blurted, "I'm only half-sorry."

He turned on the radio and she took the hint.

They drove on for a while to the rhythm of the music and the sound of rolling wheels on tarmac, but Michael soon became immune to these steady, calming sounds. Conditions had become perfect for introspection and so he allowed his mind to drift and the floodgates opened.

Three

On a scorching, cloudless mid-June day, a ten-year-old Michael excitedly approached his mother as she hung out washing on the line.

Engrossed in the task at hand, she ignored him. At any other time, when his father happened to be absent, she would reach out, hold him close to her chest, stroke his hair and speak kindly to him. It was something he would come to miss in those times his father would scold her for "mollycoddling" him.

At the centre of the overgrown garden stood an old oak tree which easily dwarfed all else around it, towering overhead and casting long, dark shadows across the entire property. From a sturdy branch hung a rope swing on which Michael, though only when permitted by his father, would gleefully rock back and forth.

For the time being, however, Michael was content just to watch his mother doing this simplest of tasks.

Negative emotions, such as hate, fear and jealousy, hadn't yet clouded his mind and he felt only love towards her. His father was different. Already Michael felt strangely distant from the man of the house, something which he perceived even then while standing in the shadow of the old oak to avoid burning his fair skin. Soon though, his mother finished her chores, walked over to him, placed her hand on his head and whispered softly into his ear, "Go and play, Mikey."

The garden then became not so much an overgrown eyesore, but an untamed wilderness in which fantasies could be acted out far away from the disapproving glances of his father. The only drawback was he could only play out his imagined adventures alone, as friends and schoolmates were forbidden from visiting by his father. So, he became adept at channelling his disappointment by tapping into the funhouse that was his imaginary world. It was an escape he would return to again and again well into adolescence and on into his adult life.

Young Michael was, like the man in some poem he had read somewhere, the monarch of all he surveyed. He took no time in bounding across the concrete yard and into the overgrown garden with its weeds and nettles, and knee-deep grass, and its bushes and hidey holes where he could lie flat on his back and stare up at the sky so his mind could wander. His play-acting centred around the things which filled the mind of every pre-pubescent boy: visions of himself as an adventurer, a pirate or, as was the case today, a World War Two Spitfire pilot.

It had been a good couple of decades since the end of the war and, with his father having been too young to enlist and his grandfather nowhere to be seen, Michael had had no one around to share their first-hand experiences of battle. However, even at that young age, he had read the books found in his father's study and understood the fundamental insanity of all conflicts, but also their necessity when things took a turn for the worst.

The words to convey such thoughts, however, eluded him and so, with a sigh, torn between outright daydream and his conscience, he strolled through the garden and into a clearing flanked by a river.

Michael knew if he stared hard enough and dismissed the glare of the sun off the water's surface then brown and rainbow trout could be seen swimming in the current. Most of them were juvenile but a few fully grown specimens were also present, and he was soon searching for pebbles along the riverbank, throwing each as he found it to skim across the surface of the water.

As the fish scattered, a multitude of ripples bounced sunbeams off the water and he smiled. On other occasions, as the trout were harassed by an onslaught of pebbles and stones, he witnessed them leap several feet into the air as if caught on a fisherman's hook. At other times, he stood still at the edge of the river up to his knees in the cold water with his hands and arms nestled just below the surface ready to propel any marine life to pass into the "net" of his entwined fingers onto the riverbank where they would jerk and twist in the sun. Most times, he caught hold of their scaly bodies and returned them safely back to the river but at others, he'd watch them twitch to death along the shoreline just inches away from the fast-flowing tributary where their salvation and survival lay teasingly close. Feeling both elated and remorseful for his actions, Michael would then toss the corpse back into the fast-flowing river's depths and attempt to make sense of the contradictory emotions which would inevitably follow every confusing episode.

Boys would be boys though, and Michael was no exception. Even though isolated from his peers, Michael was still subject to the millennia of evolution which could never be erased from the primitive depths of his mind. Deep down in every impulse which passed through his conscious mind, something primal and causal lurked. Instincts dark and profound had been inhibited and controlled by the demands of a society from which Michael was mostly cut off. Therefore, every encounter with the nameless "strangers" who crossed his path proved fascinating to him. Without siblings or friends to share his own internal and external worlds, his peer group lacked structure and, perhaps most importantly, personality.

Although it could at times be a drab place to live, the back garden was much more than just the sum of its parts. In autumn, trees became lookout posts to spy on enemies threatening to breach his well-defended castle of twigs, branches and dead leaves. In summer, the overgrown banks of nettles and grass replicated a great battlefield, replete with bunkers and dug-outs placed effectively along a no-man's-land of fallen timber and the stream a mighty stretch of water where U-boats and battleships fought for queen and country or resisted state-imposed fascism.

Michael relished these bouts of freedom far from the dusty books of the study and the chores his father imposed upon him on a daily basis. Here, amongst a rich cornucopia of life, Michael's imagination flourished. Sounds and images which, although childish and immature, served as a refuge from the harshness of his everyday life and, at times, even his existence. He sometimes wished for a real-life playmate and having outgrown the impulse to share his world with an imaginary friend — something his father went to great pains to discourage — he felt the weight of loneliness which accompanied his isolation. As he left the battlefield fort and open ocean of his world, he longed to have a friend.

It would have been a short walk back to the house and an even shorter one out to the shed in which his father kept his fishing tackle and rods, but Michael had been forbidden from ever crossing its threshold. Why this was, he didn't know. He would have liked to have cast his own line out into that ever-moving tributary but only when his father permitted it could he have done so. It was, Michael later suspected, another way for his father to control his young and impressionable son, but Michael was then still too young to comprehend the motives of his father's actions.

Bored with the skimming game, Michael turned his back on the river and left the clearing.

Four

The news on the radio was depressingly familiar, filled with the ongoing conflict in the Middle East, the slumping economy, murder and death. Lisa had remained silent for some time, but she now stirred and pointed to the sign "Talacre". Michael knew it as just another sandy beachside town which thrived during these summer months with its mini-arcades and mile upon mile of open coastline.

Why there? he found himself thinking but shook off this question. Maybe she had friends or family there, or maybe she was just like him, drifting from place to place, looking for a purpose in life. Perhaps she saw it as a place of release from her demons. Maybe he had spotted aspects of himself in her. After all, he'd had his own battles with addiction in his recent past, but group therapy had shown him the efficacy of the "talking cure".

However, the turning for Talacre was approaching fast and there was no time left for empathy so instead

Michael scrabbled to ask some of the basic questions which should have been addressed miles before reaching the outskirts of the town.

"Are you local?" he asked. "I can't place your accent."

Lisa, suddenly talkative, gave him a round-about answer. "I'm from all over. Mostly Wales though," she said with a playful smile.

Her smile at the mention of Wales set Michael off into a reverie about the UK's nations. He wasn't much of a flag-waver, either of the Ddraig Goch or the Union Jack, but was all too aware of the more gruesome and more triumphant events in the history of the country and found many correlations between Wales, the Welsh and the bloody histories of Ireland, Scotland and England and, due to the diligent study of the history of colonialism, the rest of the world as a whole.

"Do you have family in Talacre?" he asked.

"Part-time friends really," she sighed.

Michael knew from experience — mostly with the opposite sex but also from his own battles with addiction — and his sizeable experience of junkies, that she was lying. So, at the next junction, Michael slowed down as he decided to drive her as far as the town itself rather than leave her to make her own way on foot.

Why he did this, he didn't know. Perhaps it was due to simple loneliness or maybe, sub-consciously, he was hoping for more from her than just company. He could quite easily pick up a prostitute with the money he had, and he knew money was the only thing he had that *would* attract a woman. He was out of luck in the looks department, and he knew it well. He wasn't disgustingly overweight, unhealthy or unfit, just that God hadn't seen the need to deal him that particular ace.

Having established her lie in his mind, Michael listened half-heartedly to her describe her "affinity" with the coast while the last few miles of bypass ate away at the tread of the Celica's tyres.

For a time, he delivered affirmatives and negatives in the same deadpan tone while she prattled away about what he knew to be basically bullshit. The crap he'd been subjected to throughout his life had allowed him to develop an ability to sniff it out at its source. After fifteen miles of her chatter, Michael was thankful to pull into a carpark facing the ocean.

"You didn't have to take me all this way," Lisa said, adding a simple, "Thank you" before stepping out of the car.

Michael, despite her lies, was thankful for her gratitude and wished her a heartfelt "Good luck".

That was that, but, as he reached across to shut the passenger door, he noticed a small "baggie" of something brown lying in the recesses of the passenger seat's footwell. His instincts had been right. He could now label her a junkie and forget her, but having experienced the unpleasant aspects of a comedown, he almost called her back. He knew she'd be rattling for a fix later that day, but he might just be doing her a favour in denying her.

Life can be harsh, he thought as he pulled away from the town, soon stopping in a lay-by and disposing of what he presumed to be a small wrap of heroin in a nearby drain.

While pondering her possible addictions, Michael remembered his own youthful dalliances with drugs. He'd enjoyed the mellow sensations cannabis had provided and, perhaps surprisingly, had found that harder for him to give up than some of the class As he'd dabbled with. Heroin and cocaine had been a buzz and a half but, through expense and addiction, could quickly drain the resources required to acquire them. Many of his so-called friends and acquaintances had ended up owing hundreds to their dealers and, when it came to that, you could be left in seven different kinds of shit. Still, he'd managed to avoid all of that by getting out of the scene as early as he could. Drug therapy had been his saving grace.

Sitting in a circle with other junkies had woken him up and caused him to re-evaluate his lifestyle and ultimate purpose in life. But, even without the drugs, he had lacked purpose and direction; his current situation only served to further underline his life's lack of meaning. Here he was without a clue as to where he was headed or, in some respects, where he'd been. His reliance on fate could be depressing as he often came to view himself as a victim of circumstance wherein things tended to happen *to him* rather than through personal choice or free agency. Below the surface lay innumerable barely noticed emotions which he would only come to recognise through his actions. These would surprise and concern him when things went badly. And it didn't help the process of recognising, identifying or even recalling such emotions, that in company he was driven to hide his feelings from others, only opening up on rare occasions when absolutely necessary, such as during the "airing and sharing" sessions which were part of his drug counselling sessions years earlier.

His *numerous* counsellors, in time, began to see him as a success, both in terms of his recuperation and his changed view of the world. They had hailed him as a role model of recovery and as proof-positive of the power of their type of therapy with its aim of full disclosure, but still Michael had withheld a few things. Sometimes his secrecy was about maintaining personal integrity, away from intruders that sought to penetrate his whole being. At others, unless specific questions were asked about past actions or mental states, he wasn't so forthcoming about certain details. And sometimes it just hurt too much to go back there, returning him to that vulnerable state of childhood from which he, in some ways, had barely moved on from.

However, he thought this was somewhat normal. Everybody had skeletons in their closets and he was sure certain memories, which would only really surface in his dreams, he would take to his grave just as his mother had.

After the passing of a couple of hours and back on autopilot, he noticed the sign for a cafe off some rural road. Michael drove until his body and mind fought feelings of hunger and loneliness. Unlike Lisa though, he couldn't blame narcotics for his lonely condition because he would rather feel alone than used, and he had experienced the disappointment and pain of both. People had taken advantage of his easy-going manner and his reluctance to assert himself. True, his attacks on the school and persistent escapes into drugs — or now, his hitting the road — would suggest the workings of a more complicated soul. But still, he remained naive and trusting. He repeatedly expected others to treat him well. Seldom was he able to divine their motivations and he would seek solace in solitude or ruminate on philosophical fantasy when they disappointed him, protecting himself inside a snail's shell of his creation. He would become defensive, aggressive or — as the arson proved — violent. Or pathologically ruminate.

Part of Michael's difficulty with asserting himself lay in his attitude towards anger. For him, it was only ever corrosive. He would rather suppress his fury until the opportunity to release it presented itself. In his earlier years, this had meant throwing pebbles in a stream. More recently, it had involved destroying inanimate objects and torching buildings. So rarely did he express it that others started to consider him weak. For the unscrupulous, he became an easy target. He had encountered many such characters in his lifetime. He wondered whether this had been the root of his pleasure in watching the trout twitch to death along the riverbank. It was sad and cruel, but the source was the corrosive, sadistic influence of others. Deep thinking and the mind-altering effects of the drugs, whose consumption eventually became a lifestyle choice, conspired to make him reflect on the causes and effects of not just his behaviour and decisions but also of those who shared a place in his life. However, his highly introspective nature would often cut him off from the "here and now" and caused him to daydream away a large proportion of his waking life. The sudden bellow of a horn pulled him out of his thoughts and reality hit hard as he realised he'd changed lanes without checking his mirrors. The truck driver behind made the familiar wanker gesture, as Michael increased his speed and shifted into the far lane.

He was hungry now. He'd covered a hundred miles and crossed an entire county since picking up Lisa. A sign read that the next service station was another ten miles away, so he ignored the speed limit and gunned the engine.

He arrived at some cheap cafe where, while he waited for his order, the waitress pressed him into conversation on the weather and the lack of trade. He was surprised to discover she was also a part-time philosophy student, but Michael responded to this with an indifference that even he found striking. His experience with the study of that branch of academia had failed to strike a chord as his personal introverted philosophy proved more than capable of filling any such need. The waitress left him to eat and silently chastise himself for his curt reaction to her attempts at conversation. He dismissed such thoughts, and his only focus became the fry-up he was eating to feed his hunger. Despite the unhealthy nature of his choice of nourishment, he made quick work of devouring it, leaving only the plate's pattern on its surface.

With his stomach now engaged in the act of digesting a rather large meal, Michael paid up and felt better about himself by leaving a very healthy tip by way of apology for his brash behaviour. After all, on top of his rudeness, Michael was all too aware waitresses were paid peanuts.

Back inside the car, he found himself in a transient state of mind, torn between continuing his journey to some unknown destination and giving the Celica's engine time to cool.

He chose the latter and was soon returning to a point in time which began with a familiar memory of him swinging back and forth on the rope swing attached to the old oak tree which both dominated and obscured the yard and garden of his childhood; rocking backwards and forwards as far as it would allow and praying for some sort of retribution.

At the age of ten, he shouldn't have been able to understand the meaning of the word but being forbidden friends to share his world with, his attention had been directed towards books and the knowledge they imbued, which provided him with a perspective far beyond his years.

His father had ordered Michael out of the house hours ago to give him the freedom to hand his wife another beating, but Michael had still been able to hear the screams coming from the downstairs lounge, although they had now quieted into whimpers.

He felt angry. However, he hardly ever expressed the emotion to either of his parents. He still looked up to his father, or at least obeyed his demands, and at times even imitated his behaviour. Conversely, for his mother, he expressed nothing but love and compassion. He sensed hatred for his father for obvious reasons, but his mother's inaction was, for him, a source of repressed anger which allowed his negative feelings to fester and multiply. Perhaps when he was older, he would change his opinion of his dad, but he doubted it. All he felt now was the fear and anger he knew he needed to hide in order to remain sane.

In later years, he might come to understand that his mother's relationship with his father was deeply conflicted, and that she too was being conditioned by the abuse.

He found himself thinking of some future time when he wasn't weak and helpless; a day when he could enact revenge upon his father. But that day would be a long time in coming because, even after countless beatings, his mother had warned him off retaliation so as not to "lower" himself to his father's "level".

Michael, at that young age, had failed to grasp the concept though. Turning the other cheek seemed like an insanity to him despite his mother's preachings from the "Good Book" and her long lectures on morality. At that time, Michael judged it hypocritical of her to be seeking God's forgiveness for her husband and yet cursing his name after every "punishment" he inflicted on her. It made no sense to him.

In the meantime, still swinging gently beneath the branch of the oak tree, Michael was content to live inside his head for just a few minutes more while he built up the courage to re-enter the prison he called home. His thoughts remained focused on his shortcomings and deep-rooted insecurities.

He was putting off venturing inside as he always hated seeing his mother after one of his father's "episodes". If he left it a few more moments, she would be licking her wounds whilst attempting to hold back her tears, but thankfully past the worst of it. Michael decided to adopt what he saw as her stiff upper lip attitude.

At school, whether he or some other unfortunate was the victim, observation helped him rise above the physical abuse. It helped him make sense of what he came to view as a human zoo at which his attendance was compulsory. Even at this age, he saw — in children's parents — the source of their offspring's copied bullying and the insecurity inherent in such behaviour and the low self-esteem it generated.

Although social interaction did have its positive outcomes — companionship, intimacy and fun —

Michael's negative experiences, both at home and at school, meant he turned away from everyone else. In fact, he relished being alone.

Apart from it offering time to process the emotions he was subjected to, his isolation also allowed him the space to find solace in reading, and he borrowed every book he could from his father's extensive library. Reading was one of the few things which his dad approved of and encouraged and so being literate and educated had become the only tangible thing he had in common with his father. Indeed, Michael always looked forward to their long talks about every aspect of life. This only happened when his father felt the inclination to attempt some form of paternal bonding and the emphasis was always academic rather than physically affectionate or playful. Michael was better able to contain any negative thoughts towards him at these times as — apart from enjoying them — he was slow to extinguish the hope that they represented a change in attitude both to himself and his long-suffering mother.

Eventually, in a decade or so, his father would finally call time on his abusive behaviour by leaving the family home. But for Michael, neither his father's absence nor time itself proved to be a healer.

High above the oak tree, a group of blackbirds issued guttural caws, interrupting Michael's reflections, as they marked their respective territories. Michael began to cry as he got to his feet and walked back to the house. His father had left, so, pushing open the back door, he crossed the kitchen and went into the living room where his mother was also weeping, silently, in a corner of the room. She seemed about to dismiss him but must have seen the tears in his eyes and so beckoned him over. There they stayed until their tears had dried up and raindrops began to slam against the patio doors. His mother picked herself up and headed into the conservatory to watch the storm.

Alone, afraid and confused, Michael lay on the living room floor in the foetal position and began to realise this loneliness arose from his simultaneous adoption and rejection of his mother's need for solitude after marital abuse. She needed privacy at those times, like any animal in pain. He knew that and yet he still needed to be close to his mother to try to comfort her. But, despite her refusal to let him take care of her, however briefly, being close to her also made him feel vulnerable. Her soothing embraces would have made him feel weak and immature.

Such thoughts were perceived solely at the intellectual level while his emotional maturity was still far from developed. The truth was he would sacrifice all his hard-earnt intellect and perceptive thought for one perfect moment of all-encompassing happiness.

But happiness had become an alien concept to him and in the few short years prior to puberty, his own sexual awakening and his first tantalising experiences of masturbation — which his father declared sinful even before such urges had begun to manifest themselves — Michael's pre-pubescent world felt empty, but that emptiness began to dissipate in the days before his fourteenth birthday.

That was when his mother had taken a "tumble" down a narrow flight of stairs. As a witness to the "accident", Michael had ceased to see the world as an adventure. Instead, it had become a cruel place where dangers could arise as much from the social world as one's emotional interior. In the balance, he'd learnt, lay a person's sanity.

His mother, having been tormented for years, had then suffered the final episode of violence from her husband. *Was it remorse that made my father leave*? Michael wondered. *Was it guilt?* Could a character such as his father be a candidate for redemption?

Five

After a quick bite and an unproductive short encounter with an over-friendly waitress, Michael was back at the wheel. He started to think again about Lisa, the hitchhiker, and what might have led to her poor life choices. During their short time together, might he have laid the groundwork for her redemption? Saving her from herself with a small dose of the "talking cure" with which, thanks to his past vices, he was now extremely familiar.

For a while, he thought about his mother. Her legacy had been the development within him of a deep-seated liberal and philosophical outlook which also invited a feeling of compunction. Was it this trait that had acted as a catalyst to his dad's eventual sweet desertion of both mother and son? In Michael's eyes, the jury was still out on this important and very personal question.

Thoughts of Lisa's affliction were replaced by the need to find himself somewhere to rest his head, have a drink, and sleep off the unfortunate hangover which would sure as hell follow yet another one of his binges. A sign pointed to a Ramada hotel just off the bypass, and within thirty minutes he'd arrived, checked-in and was soon taking the lift up to his floor.

Nobody was around and Michael hoped there would be no stag or hen parties. It was on the edge of a town, but beyond the view from the window, it held no interest to him. He decided to call room service for a sandwich but, as he picked up the receiver, he noticed the drinks menu.

Ordering a Glenfiddich over ice, he decided the receptionist's voice sounded disapproving and so he decided not to tip. People should mind their own business. Like he did. He switched on the television and flipped through channels before settling on the shopping network. It was simple easy viewing geared towards bored housewives, but Michael found it refreshing and uncomplicated. He'd watch the adult channels later out of habit.

A knock on the door signalled the arrival of room service. Michael got out of his chair and collected his snack and drink, carrying them to the desk while his visitor took the hint and left. He ate, drank and was soon spread-eagled on the bed.

For a while, he stared up at the ceiling in his better-than-average hotel room as the television droned on.

Slowly, everything began to blur, and he closed his eyes on the world and switched off his over-active mind. He saw himself some twenty-five years younger, sliding his bed and bedroom furniture up against the door of his room. He was crying and shaking — partly in fear, but mostly out of anger. He had just witnessed his mother being struck time and again in the face, neck and torso. His father had apparently suspected an unwanted pregnancy and had punched her solidly in the abdomen, forcing her to double-up on the living room floor and sink to her knees. Once again, it seemed, something had "pressed his buttons" and he had reacted with violence before sending Michael to his room. This time though, Michael had noticed bleeding between his mother's legs and she then had let out a shrill and savage scream which only attracted contempt and anger from her husband.

His dad was in a distorted state of mind. He was intoxicated and dismissive of the pleadings of Michael and his mother. The man was unreasonable and highly psychopathic, and — for the first time in a long time — Michael actually feared for his life.

From his refuge, Michael heard his dad, still angry and drunk, climb the stairs to kick and shoulder the heavy oak door behind which he was sheltering. He would undoubtedly sober up before it would yield but Michael had become used to such behaviour, although this was the first time he could accurately label his dad a murderer.

His dreamscape altered as he found himself running through the high grass and weeds of the garden towards the river. The swing rocked violently as a gale-force wind blew in from the west, shedding leaves from the nearby trees which danced around him in an uncoordinated ballet. Michael shielded his eyes against the wind as he sprinted away while his heart beat time with his feet. He tripped on a branch and landed full force in the main corridor of his old primary school where the screaming of the wind was replaced by the sound of cane on palms and cries of pain emanating from the headmaster's office.

Derisory laughter came from his left as the older children queued up, but for Michael it was more than the anticipation of physical pain which upset him. A little bit of his resolve would be taken away with every stroke. Another piece of his soul snatched away by a sadistic and delusional old man known only by his harsh methods of discipline. He prayed for some sort of intervention but had learnt God wasn't much of a listener and acts of kindness, even shown by his own peer group, were rare.

The third hand on the old wall clock counted down while he waited outside, tears streaming down his face. He was on his knees, but adrenaline kept him from collapsing altogether onto the slate floor. Pretty soon, it was his turn. He wiped the tears from his eyes as he entered the headmaster's office and prepared to face the old bastard. The first blow he hardly felt but he was soon weeping outright as the strokes increased in frequency and intensity. He stood firm though as he knew that doubling over would just attract more strokes for not taking his punishment "like a man". His misdemeanour had been the minor infraction of leaving his shoelaces undone, but when it was over, the tingling in his palms accompanied him all the way down the corridor which serviced the main teaching block.

Michael passed through the corridor quietly so as not to disturb the upper classes studying for their exams. He made his way into the part of the school which was reserved for the "troubled" children but troubled didn't necessarily mean thick because he was, in intellectual terms, well ahead of the game. His main problem, and one for which he was frequently reprimanded, was his poorly controlled impulse to show off knowledge, although those punishments were generally meted out on the playground by his less studious classmates.

He took his time passing through the old cloakroom which smelt strongly of damp thanks to the coats left to drip on the tiled floor following a severe early morning downpour. Michael's pace reflected his anxiety about disturbing classes at study but also because he had always found this part of the school eerily calm despite the frequent cries of unruly children.

He was running by the time he entered the older part of the school. After a few moments, he tried to compose himself. Thankfully he had been alone when he had made his mad dash, so he was unlikely to face ridicule for it, but there were plenty of other jibes which he'd be subjected to that day. As he left the older part of the school and the creepy cloakroom behind, he did his best to catch up with his own breathing.

He tried to compose himself while he entered his designated-by-bad-luck classroom. Sitting himself down, he stared straight ahead, avoiding all eye contact. The chalkboard seemed to be written over with an insane amount of useless information. He'd have been much happier sitting by himself in an empty room with a copy of one of Orwell's or Hemingway's literary feasts. You could learn a hell of a lot about life within the pages of a book, once other distractions — such as the bullying of teachers and pupils — were removed. Bullying caused anxiety, and that affected his concentration. The teachers didn't seem to notice this link though, coming instead to the conclusion that his attention span was close to zero. He knew the punishment he had just received had really been as much due to a poor appraisal of his subjects across the board as it had been for his shoelaces.

This was why, it occurred to him in his dream, he was still stuck in the bottom set of every class. He also knew — as he had known as a child — that he was intelligent but that the stresses of school life impaired his focus. As his tutor, tired with the prevailing incompetence of his class, droned on about fractions and percentages while knowing full well he was largely wasting his time, Michael entered a daydream within a dream.

He found himself sitting on the edge of the riverbank just a few yards from his father's out-of-bounds tool shed. He imagined himself getting up, strolling over to its sturdy wooden door and kicking it open before barging it with his shoulder to bring the rusting hinges away altogether.

Leaning up in the back corner and glistening in the sunlight lay treasures comprising every sort of rod needed for every type of fishing. Rod rests, reels, landing and keep nets and all else a committed angler would hope to have. Starting to explore, he brushed against spider webs hanging from the wooden ceiling. The fibres ghosted his face and caught in his hair, rigid enough to entrap the occasional unfortunate insect but nothing but an annoyance to him. He reached out towards the treasure trove standing in a shadowy corner and grasped hold of the nearest rod. It was a telescopic construction which would extend roughly six feet from its base to tip. A coarse fishing reel was affixed to the handle. Michael stood, staring down at the dusty old floor, letting his mind drift even further afield. He closed his eyes, inhaling the musky scent of old wood and listening to the babble of the river just beyond. He felt alive in there, more alive than in his "real" location: a stuffy old classroom in the middle of a winter's morning.

The setting for his fishing fantasies was always a sunny summer's day. He would cast a line out onto that meandering tributary and wait for what seemed an age until the tip of his rod began to twitch with the twisting panic of a brown or rainbow trout intent on shedding the steel hook embedded in its mouth.

As he reeled it in, he anticipated and re-lived the twisted satisfaction of watching a fish twitch to death on the riverbank. Truth was, he relished the thrill of being in control of something unrelated to the complicated actions and reactions of human existence.

Michael shook off the daydream of his father's tool shed from within his adult dream of a pressure house school day. Back in the now, it was a dark night in a plush hotel room with the television on.

He tuned himself back into reality, far away from that dreaded trip to the headmaster's office, his mad dash and his short surreptitious jaunt into the fantastical, which he had enacted inside his dad's "precious" but out-of-bounds shed.

It had just passed seven and the shopping channel was flogging rings. The sour taste of whisky made him want to gag though so he drank deeply from the freebie water bottle.

His current dilemma was prosaic enough. Stay in his room or pop down to the bar? The bar won. Switching off the TV and picking up his key, he took the stairs down to reception. Things were quiet in the bar, but as long as the bartender served until eleven, everything inside his own jaded little version of the world would be just fine.

Sitting on one of the stools, he told the bartender to charge the tab to his room and sat back with a pint of Brains. The beer was cool, crisp and heavy. The barman was clearly bored and within a minute or two, he began drumming up a conversation. First was the weather, then the lack of trade.

Michael cut the discussion before any personal questions could be asked. Only slightly drunk, he decided to make a date with the mini bar in his room and so made his excuses. He was soon back in his room nursing a glass of whisky while a cheap porn film played out in the background.

Michael began chain-smoking. The past few days would be considered, in anybody's estimation, extremely stressful. A father's death, a house clearance and sale, an act of trespass and arson, all of which had triggered nights of re-lived school-set trauma, days of drifting at high speed, mentally repeating old mistakes of drug use and family dysfunction. And yet he felt removed from every minute of it.

Taking his glass and a miniature of whisky to the window, he sat and watched the lights of the town until his glass needed a refill. It was close to nine, but he had never developed an awareness of his own sleepiness. He seemed somehow as divorced from his body as he was his feelings and, as night approached, alcohol was his only ally in that necessary shift from consciousness to sleep. Michael's only plan was to drink glass after glass of spirits and watch porn until either the drink or the permitted time allowance ran out. These superficially stimulating, superficially risk-taking activities flipped in function through the act of repetition. Thrill, on repeat, becomes numbing. Staying awake was a chore and he was soon flat-out, though still fully clothed, on the hotel bed.

He slept fitfully. Unconsciously repeating the trance state induced by the alcohol and porn, his body approached something similar to a nocturnal seizure and he began rocking back and forth while a new dream took charge of his story.

Back in his teens, Michael was awakened by the sound of his mother screaming. It was coming from the upstairs landing and she was falling. He listened to each impact on every step. There had been a disagreement. He hadn't heard that part, but his father must have lost his temper. As he always did.

In future years, his mother would deny being pushed. She would flatly state she had simply lost her footing, but for Michael it was a moot point. His father's anger and violence, and the way he projected blame onto his family every time he encountered an emotion he could not recognise or own, ensured Michael would always make the facts fit the same picture. As did the look of guilt in his father's eyes the next morning. That dust-mote of recognition would eventually lead to the old man's departure: a turning point in the lives of Michael and his mother.

But in the few months following the incident, anger set in. It was a feeling which frequently seeped into Michael's dreams and psyche, and it did again now as much as it had back then. That same night when he should have been sleeping but had been woken by the shrieks of his mother echoing around the dark recesses of the house. Michael turned to the wall. Night terrors, sleep paralysis. A desire to fight his father frustrated by the immobility of sleep.

In an early hours state of fear, he always found himself searching for the source of his terror even though, deep down, he understood it existed not within his dimly lit room but inside his head, feeding off his insecurities, hates, fears, worries and doubts. There was something deeply disturbing about this kind of epiphany but no tonic could coax or mediate his demons to the point of surrender or submission.

Michael realised he possessed limited resources for dealing with it and he would have to accept the fact life itself could be harsh and filled to the brim with disappointment, such as the conflicted attitudes that had begun to systematically erode the memories of the loving relationship he had shared with his mother. Lack of direction and assertiveness in his present life lay like a fog over the past, distorting meaning and memory.

More fog. Blackout.

Six

Michael woke early, looking forward to a dose of strong coffee.

Down in the breakfast room, he drank cup after cup until he felt wired enough to drive. Within thirty minutes, he'd checked out and was back sitting behind the wheel of his car. He sat there a moment trying to figure out where he could go next and decided to keep going east all the way across the border into Cheshire and then maybe north towards Blackpool.

That wouldn't be an all-day drive so maybe he'd check out the sights after booking into a local B&B. He hated heights and so wouldn't bother with the tower or any of the amusement rides, but planned to take a walk along the seafront with the intention of looking like any other tourist.

He had been to Blackpool as a kid when his parents had insisted on him taking him. Rollercoasters, bumper cars and merry-go-rounds. He'd hated it but had forced himself to smile through each and every swerve and slide. His father's lack of empathy and reliance on social norms meant he would force his son into whatever behaviour he thought appropriate in public. Michael had inherited his dad's trigger-happy emotional system, meaning his negative emotions would soar and were searing. From his mother, he appeared, paradoxically, to be easy-going and would yield rather than assert himself.

Shaking his head, Michael switched on the radio and turned the volume up high. Heavy bass shook the car and vibrated throughout his entire body, bringing his attention back to the present. He was nearing the coast; the smell of salty seawater permeated the air.

He breathed it in, noting the wind was blowing fiercely onto the left-hand side of his car, rocking it slightly as Blackpool's urban sprawl of caravan parks and holiday lets came into view.

To kill time until he could book himself a room, Michael followed the hypnotic tick of the road's middle markers and the redundant in daylight cat eyes as he allowed his thoughts to drift.

Retrospection followed.

Seven

On the morning of his thirteenth birthday, Michael took a drag from a cigarette which he had pilfered from a pack his parents shared. The smoke slowly dissipated, and he watched as it drifted out of his bedroom window into the clear summer air. If caught, Michael knew he'd be in big trouble, especially with his father, who hypocritically smoked a pack and a half a day.

Michael had tried his first smoke a few days earlier, resulting in him throwing up in the bowl of the nearest toilet after the first few drags. A dizzy and light-headed reaction got him wondering why anyone would bother to persist with it as a steady and potentially fatal habit. But, after his fourth or fifth in as many days, its effect had become just a light state of vertigo and a stimulating high followed by a feeling of relaxation and well-being. So, this was what it meant to be addicted. And not just chemically.

It would become a twenty-five-year habit which he just couldn't kick. Having gone cold turkey a few times in the past, he knew he would have sold his own soul to satiate the extreme cravings he felt each time he took a break from smoking. His nicotine-starved bloodstream would lead to a state of irritability and petulance where even the smallest thing would anger and upset him.

Continuing to kneel at his bedroom window, smoking the last half of the cigarette, he watched and listened for any sign of movement coming from the driveway. He was all alone in the house, perched in his lookout over the main and side doors. When his parents did return, they would be together since his father forbade his wife from venturing out alone. Their weekly shopping trip generally took at least another hour and so Michael had more time to smoke, but he dared not take any more from the pack. He strolled to the bathroom, tossed the butt into the bowl, urinated and watched as what remained of his fix disappeared down the drain.

He sighed as he returned to his room and made sure the one and only window was fully open before crashing out on his bed while he waited for his parents to return. Michael knew that, as it was his birthday, there would be plans for candles and cake. He would be expected to blow out every flame as an act of yearly pretension, then feign joy and surprise as he was presented with his neatly-wrapped presents.

He just could not separate his parents' behaviour towards each other — though his father was to blame — from what he assumed was an equally conflicted attitude to their son as he achieved his childhood milestones. Being forced to act out the role of a happy family. For Christmas, Easter, New Year and all three of their birthdays. His father's birthday was the worst, since Michael would find himself sitting with a fake smile, toasting to his dad's health, wishing him a long and happy life while secretly wishing the bastard would die young.

Seeing the car outside, Michael swallowed his emotions while sucking on a breath mint and ventured downstairs into the hallway to face the annual pantomime. Even though he mentally mocked the way his parents marked his milestones, the fact was he had entered a slow transition out of boyhood. Having started to experience adolescent dreams, the breaking of his voice was inevitable, though no less embarrassing for that. And with these changes came emotional turmoil.

The "average" teenager usually just rebelled, but for Michael, rebellion was only a small part of the story. Unlike the troubled paternal relationships endured by many other teenagers, Michael had good cause to develop what his father had labelled an "attitude problem". Perhaps it was because his mother modelled an exceptional tolerance for difficult behaviour, but

Michael found it nigh-on-impossible to challenge either parent or peer. Instead, like his mother, he turned his confusion inwards. Unlike her, he found a streak of masochism growing inside him.

This streak was very likely the source of his future involvement with life-threatening substances and mind-altering drugs. There must, after all, have been an element of rebellion in his drug-taking because it was the kind of counter-culture expression of which his authoritarian father strictly disapproved. However, Michael found it hard to admit such habits could be traced directly back to his father.

He was nearing the outskirts of Blackpool now. Before long, he had checked into a B&B and embarked upon another session, wasting what remained of his day and night watching boring repeats on his claustrophobic room's television and drinking malt whisky until the very early hours.

That night though, there were no more dreams and reflections. Perhaps his mind had grown tired of its unwelcome and frequent jaunts into the fantastical, frequently nightmarish brand of his slumber-induced recollections. *Or maybe*, Michael supposed, *I've numbed my brain into complete and utter surrender.*

Whatever the reason for this rarity, the next morning, Michael found himself strolling along the extensive beach. He popped into an arcade and, later on, drank at a local bar. Eventually, he found himself bored and lonely, lying on his bed, staring up at the ceiling and trying not to think of anything in particular in a sudden, but mild form of amnesia.

Michael sighed. His home was now a seedy B&B, the first he had found the previous day. It was quiet enough; no one had hassled him, but he was bored. Maybe he'd take another walk along the beach and listen to the crash of the waves as he stared out across the Irish Sea.

It was early August, and the illuminations were due to be switched on. Like a big kid, he'd probably attend, but there were still a few hours to kill between then and now. Without bothering to wash, he got up, slipped on his trainers, picked up his jacket and stepped out into the corridor. Down the stairs he went and out into the messy, overpopulated town that was Blackpool.

Heading for the seafront, he noticed the lights, which would be undergoing their final checks before the big switch-on tonight. The screeches of people high on adrenaline and hysteria, coming from one of the rides nearby, were escalating; emotions which hardly ever affected him. Even during his arson attack on the school, apart from a slight feeling of trepidation and a bout of unrestrained elation, he had kept his cool. In any case, trundling along on a track on one of the tallest rollercoaster rides in Europe and facing a thirty-mile-an-hour descent didn't really register with him as being any kind of fun. So, whilst this ride twisted and turned through yet another chicane in the track, eliciting a bout of high-on-adrenaline screams from its occupants, Michael smiled a nervous smile.

This smile was not dissimilar to the sadistic grin his dad had sported on many occasions and many years earlier. As he caught a reflection of himself in a ticket booth window, he became aware of the close physical likeness between the two.

Michael sighed and averted his gaze. Then, because even these similarities seemed to have demonstrated the ability to alter and depress his mood, he tried to focus on anything other than these malign, intrusive thoughts. Surrounded by the shouts and screams of thrill seekers, he couldn't organise his emotions and found himself thinking back to the countless beatings he had suffered at the hands of his father and was soon wondering why he had come here at all. The amusements, arcades and rollercoaster rides seemed to have triggered his agitated state. Things were also loud and brash, and Michael soon wished he was somewhere far away from this part of the town.

There was quite a crowd at the pier but past the stalls and amusements he was glad to see it thinned. Placing his hands on the safety rail, he looked out to sea and wondered what would happen if he decided to jump. He guessed he'd probably get pulled out of the water by the coastguard and ferried to the local asylum, but there were first times for everything.

He continued to stroll along the promenade, taking in the sights of the afternoon: the hazy sunshine, light drizzle and the crashing of the waves all along the length of Blackpool's coastline.

He drifted further away from the main drag, found a small cafe and ordered a drink. For a while, he felt peaceful but found himself remembering an incident with his father. It had included a botched attempt at sea fishing before they had headed back to a holiday chalet which, although weather-beaten, was still standing further along the same stretch of beach he'd casually strolled along for the best part of an hour the previous afternoon.

Such memories served no purpose aside from darkening his mood so even in his most peaceful moments, Michael often found himself resurrecting the negative aspects of his life. His mood had morphed into negatives and now he was hungry. He ordered himself a late brunch and nursed a cup of tea while patiently waiting for his food.

He remained agitated and was now in an anti-social frame of mind, wanting only to eat and head back to the B&B, which was now his temporary home and where, at some point, he would drink these nagging thoughts away.

His food arrived surprisingly quickly given the amount of trade and he was soon making short work of it, forgetting the table manners which he'd been taught to adopt during childhood. He found it liberating to ignore old habits and break the rules of convention.

Having cleared his plate, he paid his bill along with a small tip, and headed back to the B&B for a shower and a change of clothes.

He felt better afterwards, calmed and with negative thoughts kept at bay. It was one o'clock and still too early to start drinking so he lit up a cigarette and switched on the television, looking for a film or a documentary to entertain him. He soon found what he wanted on channel two, an old black and white movie, the name of which escaped him.

He sat there for an hour or so when a knock on his door interrupted the plot of the film and broke his concentration. Slightly agitated, Michael opened his door to find it was one of the other residents; a temporary neighbour, tall and gaunt, asking for a cigarette.

"Can I cadge a smoke?" he slurred, as if slightly inebriated.

Michael offered him the half-empty pack.

"I'm Chris, by the way. From across the hall," the neighbour added.

Michael shook his hand but only because Chris had offered it. He felt uncomfortable doing so because, having been one himself, he could easily spot a heroin addict.

"You're a diamond," Chris said, taking the last of Michael's smokes.

Hepatitis, and quite a few other "nasties" were a risk, so Michael quickly ended the brief exchange by closing the door on Chris.

Although feeling like a sucker, Michael found he now had something to do. Slipping on his jacket, he made his way outside in search of the nearest off-licence or corner shop. Finding one at the end of the next street, he got himself a large bottle of whisky along with the couple of packets of cigarettes he'd primarily come for. Getting back to his room, he found himself pouring a generous measure of Scotch into a glass.

Draining it, he quickly developed a thirst, drinking shot after shot until around five when, with the room spinning around him, he passed out, rather unceremoniously, on his bed.

Eight

For a while, his mind remained blank and Michael found himself grateful for the reprieve. It was short-lived though. Through some sort of random association with his present location, his thoughts conjured memories, focused primarily on his very first rollercoaster ride and its embarrassing and ultimately violent consequences.

Still in Blackpool, but as a boy again, he found himself sitting at the gates of a ride on a sultry day at the beginning of a week's family holiday. A sturdy bar was locked in place across his chest. He was frightened and the ride hadn't even started.

Adrenaline coursed through his body, making him shake. He repressed an intense need to scream. His father was watching, and any outward appearance of trepidation would only land him a beating.

The ride started and the rollercoaster steadily built up speed as it twisted around the first corner, slowly progressing towards its apex before a hundred-foot vertical drop. Within seconds, it was teetering at the brink. Tears filled his eyes and a scream erupted. His body was racked with tremors and, despite his best efforts, the rollercoaster made its rapid descent into yet another chicane.

He felt something warm and wet seeping into the space between his legs. For the first time in years, Michael had wet himself. Panic set in when he began to understand what this would mean to his father: his weak and weedy son had pissed himself in front of a crowd. Michael knew that not only would he be subjected to his father's anger, but so too would his mother, who was constantly accused of babying her son, showing compassion whenever he cried or, in this case, embarrassed himself.

Despite this though, and even though he couldn't see him clearly, Michael knew that beneath him his father would be smiling widely, seemingly delighted by this latest opportunity to display violence. It was some perversion.

Could his dad love at all? Was all strong feeling covered by alcohol and rage? Was its source Michael's own grandfather? The man Michael would never meet, whether because of death, estrangement, or family orchestration. There had even been hints dropped by Michael's mother — and his father when drunk — that the man had rejected Michael's grandmother, presumably showing the bullying attitude the family always displayed towards its apparently weaker but, in reality, more emotionally capable and expressive members. It was all a sick merry-go-round of violence and fear which Michael was certain would end with him. Whether such a viewpoint was accurate or not, he'd never know because he wasn't inclined to gamble, especially not with other people's lives and also sometimes not even with his own. This was, he had realised, the primary reason for his single and childless status in the present.

Embroiled once again in the memory, Michael could now see the last corner of the track and was relieved as his carriage slowed and eventually stopped at the exit gates. He got up slowly, his hands covering his crotch and his face as red as sunburn. Instantly, his father knew something was amiss. He reached for his arms and pulled them apart to reveal his damp shorts. His mother gasped.

They then began the half-mile walk back to their chalet; Michael fighting to keep pace with his father as he was dragged along the shoreline, through the bustling funfair, onto the promenade and then along the beach. Turning slightly inland, they neared their temporary home. Michael fought back the tears while seagulls cawed above, fighting over scraps of food while his dad grunted in exertion and anger. He was also muttering to himself — a habit which Michael had observed before.

That half-mile walk passed far too soon as his left arm threatened to pull away out of its socket and his heart skipped several beats, causing him to gasp as much air as he could.

Soon they had arrived back at the steps of the chalet. His father pulled out a large bunch of keys and unlocked the door as Michael's mother stroked his hair and uttered a silent prayer for her son.

Inside, the chalet was furnished cheaply and sparsely. Michael's father unbuckled his belt and applied it with some force to his outstretched hands. Pain for him was only part of the ordeal. It was the same experience as at school; punishment was as damaging to self-esteem as it was to the physical body.

Michael felt weak and helpless; he was sobbing even harder now despite his father's disapproving comments. It was then that he delved deep into his inner world as he brought to the front of his mind an image of the cool running water of the stream at the back of his childhood home. The thought of the flowing waters calmed him, releasing his mind away from the emotional hurt and his body from the physical pain as stroke after stroke of leather and steel met skin.

He dreamt unfulfilled dreams and wishes while stuck like glue to the chalet's cheap carpeting. But still his visions didn't quite shut out his own and his mother's anguish. Eventually, the ordeal came to an end. Having been ordered out of his father's sight to contemplate his "disgusting" actions, Michael lay, recovering, on the mattress of the spare bedroom. Thankfully, his father proceeded to storm out of the chalet, undoubtedly heading for the nearest public house.

Lying there, Michael supposed he must love his dad, despite everything. He had so little to recommend him as a role model that he supposed this attachment must somehow be hard-wired. But it was only a matter of time before some other petty circumstance led to another of his father's "episodes".

There were periods when his mother and he would forget these stress points despite their bodies' bearing the physical reminders of previous outbursts. All they needed to do was look down on their own hands, arms or faces. Easier to overlook were the psychological scars: anxiety, anticipation, the avoidance of certain subjects, even the expression of mild emotion. The fear of being ambushed by a gush of violence when they let their guard down to begin to live as though they were a normal family, facing the ordinary ups and downs of real life with the usual range of emotions.

A host of physical and mental sensitivities were the legacy his father would bequeath Michael and his mother when he left. For Michael, they would reinforce each other in stress signals. These old physiological symptoms would forever intertwine in his mind with situations of apparent impotence, weakness and inaction.

His dreams were often of impotence. In them, he regressed and was held captive to strong emotion. Here he was, an adult, dreaming and reliving wetting himself in front of a crowd. It wasn't just his father who had humiliated him. It was the outside world, the onlookers who he resented for not intervening, for not seeing what the family went through behind four walls. He forgot no one had known what went on beneath the social veneer. The bruises were hidden, the mental adaptations were overlooked. But that oversight added a layer of humiliation to the family's decades-long bouts of bullying.

And why had Michael and his mother never spoken out, stood up for themselves, enlisted outside support? The more isolated they had become, the more normalised the behaviour had seemed. And maybe there was a streak of fear which held them back; a domestic tyrant appeased can, on some level, be lived with.

Michael had staggered back to the B&B, drunk himself dry and was now dreaming, properly, in bed.

The dreams were less regressive now. They had moved on to those final years when he might have been able to stand up to his father; when he'd been a grown man living alone in a separate house, albeit the old family home. But all he had had was more of his dad's dominating, criticising and attempts to control him through guilt. His abuse had been systematic. In the absence of shame, it had no boundaries and there was no likelihood of it abating. No wonder Michael had become so self-destructive.

During his last years, a degree of regret had been expressed in letters sent by his father. He'd sought forgiveness from his only child. But, of those letters which he had received, Michael had either left them half-read or, more commonly, completely unopened. His father had remained as sharp as a pin till his dying breath, untouched by Alzheimer's or dementia. His antennae had stayed finely attuned to his son's weaknesses. He had manipulated Michael's own crippling emotions: his empathy, love and the potential for forgiveness. The old man saw in sensitivity, compassion and the ability to see the reasons behind abuse and forgive it, a weak person. He saw it in his wife as he saw it in his son. But he could not stand the weak person which he in fact was, and he projected a hatred of weakness onto and into those closest to him.

Sometimes, Michael had wished for siblings. Not for companionship or empathy, but just to share the brunt of his father's abuse. However, he was aware how selfish the wish was, and it often led him to doubt his own belief in treating others as he wished to be treated. Maybe he was also ultimately a bully himself?

Nine

Michael woke up with his head pounding and sickness in his belly. He rushed to the bathroom, bent over the toilet, emptied his stomach into the bowl and flushed. He rifled through his satchel and retrieved a toothbrush and a tube of toothpaste, and brushed his teeth thoroughly.

It had become dark. His watch told him it was well past nine. Looking out of the window, he saw the illuminations were shining brightly. He'd missed the switch-on but wasn't much bothered. A million glowing lightbulbs were just that. He hadn't even sampled Blackpool's classic attraction and yet the place was already getting on his nerves. Despite the time, he decided to get in his car and get out of the town as fast as he possibly could. Where he would go, he didn't know, but even sleeping in his car would be an improvement.

He had paid his bill in advance so all he had to do was re-pack his satchel, throw it in the boot and get behind the wheel. He was still slightly drunk so he hoped he wouldn't get stopped by the law.

Driving along the seafront, he passed the crowds waiting for admittance to the various pubs and clubs scattered along both sides of the road. Just seeing them made him anxious. He hated crowds, especially intoxicated ones, who were often looking for trouble or a confrontation with anyone unfortunate enough to cross their paths.

Alcohol, although regarded as a social drug, could quite easily turn the average punter into a highly unreasonable *anti*-social animal devoid of reason and responsibility. As far as he was concerned, binge-induced hangovers had endowed him with memory loss, headaches, bouts of vomiting and a series of emotional downers. All told, it conspired to make him feel like going teetotal. In theory. Habit and addictions were hard to break. Even at his lowest ebb, the thought of another drink would become less a desire and more like a need.

Drink had become a major part of his life. Manifesting itself in a fully fledged addiction barely a year after he'd first experienced its effects in early adolescence. It had remained a crutch throughout his early adulthood.

Back on Earth and only fifteen minutes out of town, Michael felt overcome by nerves and pulled into a parking lot facing the ocean. He decided to sleep in the car. Pushing the driving seat back as far as it would go, he retrieved a blanket from the back and pulled it around his shoulders while switching on the heaters. In the glove compartment sat a bottle of brandy and he was soon unscrewing its top and raising it to his lips as he watched the waves crash along the shoreline some fifty feet away. Downing the brandy like it was Coca Cola, he passed out.

Before long, he was a child again, back in Blackpool.

Ten

They had been sea fishing and Michael was left alone by his father. The trip had not gone well. His dad had deliberately disappeared into the sand dunes, leaving Michael behind. Some trigger had got him emotional again.

As Michael waited for him, he chewed on a thumbnail and kicked out at the sand beneath his feet. There had been a point when he had feared his dad was about to bare his soul to him. Had that happened, Michael would probably have ended up sympathising with the bastard, so that was some consolation.

Instead, Michael continued looking towards the crashing waves of the Irish Sea; his mind for once blank. Although highly introverted, he now found his internal world surprisingly drab and boring whereas at any other time it offered him a break from the harshness of reality with a veritable cornucopia of sounds and images.

At his feet lay all the fishing gear: rod, bait and hooks. His father had promised to show him the finer points of beach casting, so they had left his mother alone in the chalet where she was often effectively a prisoner.

He thought about casting out the line but decided against it for fear of his dad thinking him boastful. Instead, he waited for his return.

Eventually, Michael saw him appear from out of the coastal haze. His purposeful stride abandoned for once as he picked his way across the sand. Michael perceived the remnants of tears in his bloodshot eyes. Michael moved towards him, more curious than concerned, and received a full-force slap to the head. As his father picked up his fishing rod and began to leave the beach, Michael shed tears of his own. He picked up his rod and reel and followed his father off the beach.

He felt nothing much of anything. There had begun a pattern where he was almost partly, perversely, relieved by violence, as it briefly stopped the intrusive thoughts that filled his mind the rest of the time.

They returned to the small beachside carpark and, without a word, Michael gently opened the door behind the driver and sat himself inside the car quietly. Although his mother was not in her usual place in the passenger seat, his father always insisted on him riding in the back. They pulled away; his father grinning like a maniac.

In a way, Michael understood. His father had marched off on the beach in an attempt, for once, to master his emotions. His son had not been trying to rile him but had perhaps shown vulnerability as a fishing novice. But for his dad, there was some cross-wired association of strong emotion with Michael. He felt his son was to blame for the fact he felt angry. Michael was able to relate to his father's violent knee-jerk form of expression. After all, on the playground or at home, he felt a sense of loathing bubbling up inside him whenever he was in a situation where the other person seemed to have the upper hand emotionally or, conversely, showed vulnerability. Both the bully and the victim had, for him, become emotional triggers.

In the meantime though, this ticking time-bomb continued to be fuelled by the same fear and hate prevalent in his early life and, though he was no sage, he was sure it would be ever-present throughout his life.

There wasn't a chance of becoming what he hated however. He was sure of that. Aside from a few broken windows and a streak of petty vandalism in his early adolescence, Michael wouldn't witness fear in the eyes of those whom he chose to love. Nor would he have to face his fear bouncing off the walls of a prison cell followed by the despair that came along with a poor sense of judgement.

His own self-destructive tendencies would end up presenting themselves as the last mouthful of booze from yet another liquor bottle. Drink, and all of its destructive qualities, would later serve as a temporary release while a few thousand brain cells expired with each sip. The dampening influence it provided seemed well worth the sacrifice and, if he was being honest with himself, was a welcome distraction from his over-active mind. It became a habit rather than a lifestyle choice and habits, he found, tended to die hard.

From his first addiction to nicotine which he experienced through the deceit he'd shown towards his parents, the stimulants of illegal class A drugs, and the depressive qualities of alcohol had grown risk-taking behaviour and a pleasure implicit in doing something wrong.

Even if he was only hurting himself, this behaviour was also addictive. Self-destruction was, and remained, one of the sweetest forms of pleasure, and it was one in which he'd decided every human being engaged in throughout their lives. Whether it be the simple sensations that came through the misuse of drugs or the half-conscious decision to sever all bonds with your fellow men, the sensation of just letting go was a sweet kind of sorrow and one which he savoured every day of his life.

Life was cruel, unkind and unfair, and even though he'd accepted this fact, Michael refused to act vindictively towards any other person or living thing. This he left to others. Although guilty as sin of trespass and arson, try as he might, he could never seem to reciprocate physical violence or mental torture of the kind which some human beings were subjected to and challenged by. He'd learnt to turn the other cheek and inspired pride in his mother by doing so. However, the truth continued to be anything but rosy — even when viewed through rose-tinted glasses.

Eleven

Stuck in his car some twenty-five years later, Michael awoke in time to see the sunrise on the surface of the ocean. It was beautiful, making him feel better about being alive. However, his stomach warned of an imminent spasm so he leapt out of the car and ran towards the beach. He threw up along the shoreline then rubbed at his streaming, bloodshot eyes.

After returning to his car, Michael watched a jogger pounding along the beach in a sweat-stained T-shirt and high-visibility jacket. The runner turned his head and waved an awkward hello. Michael beeped his horn in response. He tried to sleep again but after half an hour spent wriggling in his seat, he gave up the ghost and decided to make his way to the nearest drive-through for a high-fat, high-calorie breakfast.

Fifteen minutes later, he'd found a service station and was soon ordering his meal through the speaker system, dictating his order to some over-worked, under-paid wage slave.

He ate in the parking lot. He made quick work of his breakfast and then made his way inside to find a toilet. Michael washed his face in the shallow sink and dried it with a few paper towels. Feeling a little refreshed, he walked back to his car and left.

Getting back onto the motorway, he drove north for as far as the petrol in his tank would accommodate. Maybe he would refuel; he still hadn't got used to the fact he now was a relatively wealthy man.

Scotland was appealing as it would take him far from the memories which had been triggered when stuck in his home country or walking the extensive shores of Blackpool. The most predictable destinations were Glasgow or Edinburgh so, taking a coin from his pocket, he flipped it in the air and waited for it to land on the passenger seat. It fell heads-up. Glasgow it was.

His libido now made him wish for a release. It wouldn't be the first time he'd hired a "working girl". As long as they were clean and gave the impression they weren't forced into it, he had no moral qualms. If he paid over the odds, even double, it assuaged what little guilt he felt after the act. He always wore protection and usually booked a hotel room as it was far safer than using his car.

It took him four hours to reach the sprawl of Glasgow's rundown outer suburbs and the dockyard chimneys and smog of Clydeside. At nearly every crossroads or traffic light junction, armed police vans seemed to share a lane with him. Michael found himself becoming paranoid. Was he over the limit? Or was there something highly illegal secreted within an inside pocket of his satchel? Something which any copper would be happy to confiscate. He began to sweat and hoped to God it wouldn't give the cops a reason to stop him.

But every police officer, positioned behind bulletproof windscreens, seemed to be more interested in the prospects of the lights changing than a sweat-stained, slightly suspicious-looking driver. They, Michael assumed, were more interested in catching gun-toting maniacs. Which struck him as ironic.

While he had committed trespass and arson, Michael somehow didn't connect the incident with the fear he now felt for the police; worrying about all of the things he hadn't done whilst the thing he *had* done remained locked away. To the best of his knowledge, there hadn't been any witnesses. Why would there be in a sleepy little town in the early hours of the morning? There certainly wouldn't be anything to forensically implicate him to his crime. The symbolic attack on his past had been completely out of character and he was sure any snippet of evidence would have gone up in smoke. *It's a shame my conflicted opinions on life refuse to do the same*, he thought.

Losing this train of thought, Michael noticed dusk had fallen whilst the urban sprawl gave way to a build-up of shops, hotels and restaurants. After booking himself into a smart city centre hotel, he went out in his car again and headed towards a rough-looking area. Winding down the passenger side window, he waited only a short while. He was seeking a woman who could pass as his wife or girlfriend as they entered the hotel, and he soon spotted a potential working girl leaning up against a lamppost.

Smiling, she came over to his car. "You after directions or something?"

Michael returned her smile. "I could do with some company."

"Okay," she replied, getting into the car.

"What's your name?" he asked as they pulled away from the kerb.

"Claire."

Michael could see Claire was even more attractive than Lisa the hitchhiker. She was average height with a nice figure, and Michael wondered why she didn't practise her trade via an escort agency rather than by walking the streets. Maybe Claire was also a junkie. He knew the agencies frowned upon that kind of thing. But on the plus side, she'd pass for an ordinary young woman, in her knee-length boots, black trousers and a faded beige top draped under a cream jacket. As Michael took in her medium-length dark brown hair, full lips and high cheekbones, he felt himself becoming aroused. But then she blurted, "Fuckin' rain!" in a strong Glaswegian accent and Michael sighed.

During the short journey back towards the hotel, he found it hard to concentrate on the road, and kept glancing at his new passenger. As they came to a halt in the carpark, Claire said, "I take it we're not going to do it in the car then?"

"Correct," he said.

They walked towards the hotel entrance hand in hand, playing the part of a love-struck couple to keep up the pretence. At the reception desk, a bored-looking clerk greeted them slackly before returning to his computer screen and a game of solitaire.

They took the lift to the second floor and strolled down the corridor towards room 201. Fishing out his key, Michael soon had the door open and the lights on. Claire seemed impressed by the plush suite. Michael headed for the mini bar where he poured them both a drink. He didn't know whether she liked whisky but poured them both a generous measure of the Scotch.

She shook her head, saying, "No thanks. I'm a Catholic."

Michael was briefly taken aback until she added, "Only joking," and swallowed the drink in one. *What the hell?* Michael thought, copying her and then pouring the equivalent of four shots into each of their glasses.

Passing her the refilled glass, he asked, "How much for the whole night?"

"You mean, how much do I make in a night-time?"

Nodding, Michael repeated, "Yes. How much for tonight?"

"One-fifty."

Michael opened his wallet. Even though flush, he shouldn't have been carrying as much as he had around central Glasgow. As he passed her the notes, Claire all but snatched them from his hands. Then, sitting on the room's only chair, she began undressing. She beckoned him over, still holding the glass in her hand. And so, while plying themselves with drink, they allowed Mother Nature to take over and ended up in a loose embrace on the bed before falling asleep.

Twelve

Once again, Michael slept, finding himself focusing on the back end of the rollercoaster and sea fishing incidents.

Having left the chalet early, they ended up sacrificing the last few days of their holiday and were soon heading home via a motorway and a plethora of B-roads which, if they had kept to their original plans, would have been swarming with traffic. As it was, most of the three lanes were quiet and looked almost abandoned. Getting back took just shy of a couple of hours as they left the coastal scenery behind and ended up passing through a stretch of wet and windy north Wales.

What had happened on the rollercoaster was still on everybody's minds. Although, on their departure and journey, his father had communicated his displeasure for once only verbally rather than physically. The incident seemed to have affected him to the point of distraction.

Michael understood his dad seemed to be emotionally tortured by some deviant element from his past.

Given his age, Michael shouldn't have been capable of such insight. In many ways, he was very immature, but he was observant, analytical and very capable of perceptive leaps. Living with his father modelling anger while his mother modelled tolerance had created a space in which he could ponder on an intellectual level. Like his mother, he had become attuned to every nuance of his father's moods, wondering what might have caused them and why. Like her, he became adept at skirting danger areas, reading his face, judging whether it was something he had said that had made him lose his temper again. They were both highly sensitive with an almost uncanny ability to read other people. He wasn't psychic but the fact remained he was gifted in a way most others of his age group, through nature or nurture, didn't seem to be. But it was tiring; something which might explain the exhaustion he frequently succumbed to during the course of an average school day.

Back in the car in his dream, he sat with his mother in silence as the scenery changed from the mundane to the familiar as they neared home, and the pace of their journey slowed as the standard of the roads deteriorated. Distant mountains loomed out of the mist and his father sighed as they pulled into their driveway.

After exiting the car, they could hear the babble of the stream which twisted and turned at the rear of the property as they unloaded two heavily packed suitcases and made their way to the front door. A neighbour waved, crows cawed from the apex of the old oak tree, and everything seemed peaceful and tranquil on the surface. Deep down though, and when he awoke in a hotel room many years later far away from his childhood home, Michael knew things had been far from normal, and for him they would remain so for the better part of a quarter of a century.

Within his first few moments of consciousness, Michael imagined he could still sense the cold crisp air and hear the low drone of suburban living, but he soon realised it was just the sound of the hotel room's air conditioning.

He turned to see whether Claire was still there, but found he was hugging a pillow. Getting up, he checked his wallet was still in the back pocket of his jeans and that no money had been taken. His wallet was fine.

He put on fresh underwear and socks and a clean shirt.

Checking his watch, he saw it was just gone ten — still early enough to get a decent breakfast downstairs. He pulled on his trainers and took the lift down to reception, turned left and got himself a table in the half-empty restaurant.

After he'd eaten, he went to pick up his satchel from his room and found the maid adding up the bill for the mini bar. He discovered it had been a very expensive evening considering the amount of booze that had been drunk and the added cost of his "entertainment" for the night. He headed for reception, paid his bill and walked to his car. He closed the door and sat there for a moment thinking about everything and nothing while the heaters killed the chill in the air.

Eventually, he came to the conclusion he had unfinished business with Claire. He felt a deep need to see her again so they could talk some more, but he also felt a similarly deep compulsion to continue his road trip north because he had begun to appreciate that, despite the familiarity of his own regressive dreams, every mile that moved him further from his childhood home had improved his mood on a mental and spiritual level.

He considered his options and decided on another night's stay. After waiting half an hour, he strolled back to the reception where he was told he would face a wait until the rooms were free for check-in. After requesting the same room, he made his way to the hotel's public bar for a pint or two to kill the time. After easily filling the three-hour wait, Michael was handed his room key at precisely two o'clock.

For a while, he considered staying at the bar but knew he was already highly intoxicated. Instead, he made his way up to his room, crashed out on the bed and spent the remainder of the afternoon sleeping with his head full of thoughts relating to the aborted trip to Blackpool and hazy recollections of unpacking his old and faithful satchel.

He was slow and deliberate, making sure not to crease the unworn trousers and shirts which his mother had washed, ironed and packed before setting off from their homestead at the beginning of the week. Even though it was his father who was obsessed with him looking "presentable", he still respected her work.

It was a dreary Thursday morning and, having returned home the previous afternoon, Michael found himself carefully hanging up the garments whilst doing his best not to let the dismal state of the weather depress him. Wind and rain pummelled his bedroom window and seemed on the verge of breaking through, but the single-paned divide proved an effective barrier between him and the extremes of the weather.

Blackpool hadn't been that different. Rainclouds had constantly threatened their "week in the sun" and, on a few occasions, they had passed overhead, shedding their loads all over the overcrowded, hyperactive town.

Michael hated being home, but at least the routine it demanded calmed him. Things were more predictable here than out in the big, wide world with its levels of insanity that exceeded even his troubled father's nonsensical philosophies on life. Routine calmed him. In fact, he had been looking forward to it, and had not really been disappointed that the holiday had been truncated.

Continuing to focus on the task at hand, he hung up his clothes meticulously, careful to preserve the state of them and mindful of the effort his mother had made in making him look presentable. Michael felt half-grateful for her care as his neat appearance helped deflect attention away from him; in school the bullies were more concerned with tormenting the scruffier kids in the playground. He was only taunted for being a weirdo. Presumably the kicks and punches he received were for the same reason, though he really didn't know.

Although he hadn't quite managed it at home, at school he had learnt to withstand physical and verbal abuse. His father had taught him bullies were rewarded by signs of their target feeling hurt. He had learnt what it meant, for some, to appear as though you were "weak". At home, he would still indulge in fits of tears or hysterical laughter. Anger though, was the emotion he sought most of all to avoid. When he did, he would make sure he was alone, unwitnessed, as he tortured some poor fish flapping about and slowly dying on the riverbank.

Michael sometimes wished he could deal out the same punishment, not only to his father, but also to the bullies who frequently verbally abused him in the playground. He'd discovered this kind of abuse could be much more emotionally draining than physical pain. The weekly bouts of kicks and punches were not what he feared the most. It was a slow, constant loss of pride and self-respect but he remained resilient to these attacks. Maybe he had his father to thank for teaching him to retain a stiff upper lip and endure what came his way like a man. The trouble was, although puberty had hit, he felt very little like the man he pretended to be whenever his father was around.

But these bouts of emotion were now half-instigated by the hormones which were beginning to circulate around his body and in his brain, causing him despair and the one emotion he strived to bury: anger.

Unfortunately, that was how Mother Nature worked. Although on a physical and emotional level, Michael was easy prey, he had brains and intellect, but most people failed to see it. In a perverse way, Michael was glad.

He was surprised to find he'd completed packing away his luggage from their little jaunt to Blackpool, but he couldn't quite recall doing so. He'd been in a waking fugue state. He had read a book on psychology from cover to cover three times over and felt well-informed on the basic tenets of the subject and such mental states but was too busy now to ponder the thought for more than a second or two. His father was calling him to lunch and, obedient as ever, Michael headed downstairs to the dining room where he took on the persona of a boy far more emotionally mature than he actually felt.

Such memories were relegated to the back-burner as Michael woke in his plush hotel room with a punishing headache. Soon, he was throwing up in the bathroom toilet. He'd drunk far too much while waiting to check in. It was six in the evening. He'd have to cut down on his drinking as it was muddying his mind.

Strong black coffee followed. TV: classic Hitchcock, *Rear Window*, starring Jimmy Stewart. Out of the window: industrial units, city centre offices, the glowing lights of Glasgow. Dream state.

Thirteen

Michael swung his legs back and forth, making the branch of the old oak tree creak with the effort of accommodating his weight. He wasn't heavy in the sense of being fat or obese though. In this memory, he was just older and therefore heavier.

He should have grown out of childish things like rope swings and daydreams but, when things got too drab or stressful, they became a good form of release.

The wind, coming in heavily from the north, pushed him backwards as it collided with his body and sent him swinging in a dizzying arch below the boughs and, despite his age, he found it exciting and pleasurable. It also took his mind off his current situation in which he'd again found himself the victim of what would become his father's final act of violence.

He'd grown rapidly in the years between childhood, adolescence and puberty and now matched his father in height, weight and intelligence. But still he feared him. A streak of cowardice compelled him to always obey his dad because, deep down, he remained a scared and confused young boy whose only form of defence was the submission of his thoughts to the fantastical.

For fifteen years he'd been mollycoddled by his mother and physically and mentally abused by his father. Unsurprisingly, he was bitter with anger, but he was also considerate and caring thanks to the loving influence of his mother.

Thoughts of her soon sullied his mood though as he switched his focus onto the times when her bumps and bruises had become so regular as to be unremarkable. But this soon struck a chord with him as he brought himself violently back to reality.

Right now though, being both fifteen in his past and…

Fourteen

Now in his late thirties, Michael tipped a glass to his lips as he continued to bathe in the glow of Glasgow and *Rear Window.* Darkness fell towards night as the final credits rolled. Flipping channels, he found there wasn't much else to focus on; a choice between the news and a John Wayne western which, with its unrealistic take on a past that never was, he knew would aggravate and bore him. However, he found himself wondering whether, despite its unrealistic plot, the world of cowboys and Indians was grounded in more fact than the news channels and their rolling sound-and-vision streams of a world gone increasingly mad.

He leant back to enjoy the comfort of the air-sprung mattress, but was bored of the confinement of his physical and mental space. At nine, after an hour of excess and a few hours of sleep, he pulled on his jacket. He needed company and wanted to talk. He decided he would try to find Claire again, hoping she could shift some of the circuits in his mind. Whether or not she'd be "working" after the previous night's windfall was anybody's guess. He kept his fingers crossed.

In the carpark, it started to rain so he flipped on the windscreen wipers and was soon heading once more towards the centre of Glasgow. Parking up in the same spot as the previous night, he waited for an hour without so much as a glimpse of her and was about to leave when he saw a woman wearing similar clothes to Claire's. It was close to ten o'clock and his stomach was demanding food. Ignoring its pangs, he tooted his horn at her and she turned.

Michael wound down the passenger side window.

"Still looking for directions?" she asked.

He smiled back at her and said, "Yeah. I've lost my way."

It was perhaps the greatest truth he'd uttered in years.

They drove back to the hotel in silence, passed by reception, and again took the lift to his floor. Michael settled back on a swivel chair while Claire sat on the bed and began to undress.

He stopped her with five words. "I just want to talk."

Claire frowned. "It's one of those gigs then."

Michael frowned too. "I'll pay you the going rate for the night."

"You must have a lot on your mind to be paying that much."

"What I have on my mind will take that long."

"Okay, any chance of a drink?" she asked.

Michael went over to the mini bar, forgetting his previous promise to cut down on the booze. He got them both a drink, this time offering a choice. She asked for vodka and tonic while he stuck to whisky. He sat and began to talk.

Recalling them in vivid detail, Michael described the most important elements of his past exploits. With anybody else, he would have felt shy and nervous but, since the sex, he felt at ease in her company. After all, she'd probably heard it all from other men, just as damaged as him. Although he was paying her for her time, he didn't expect the insight or enlightenment a psychotherapist could have offered him; all he wanted was a listener. Someone to whom he could pour out his heart, whether they were inclined to care or not.

He left out the fire at the old school. Not from fear of prosecution, but because he had already questioned his sanity at the time and felt compelled to hide this from her. Despite the torment of his school days, had he really been entitled to set the place on fire? Had he simply been blowing off steam or out to settle a score? Maybe he believed the act had been righteous revenge and, therefore, wasn't entirely wrong. Or maybe he had already begun to walk the path that ultimately led to insanity. Also, he found that keeping this secret gave him a degree of pleasure, almost as much as the act itself. When alone and his mood was low, he could relish the sights, smells and emotions of that night. It seemed to calm.

Despite his decision to conceal his visit to the school, there was still much left to reveal to Claire. From his father's beatings to the emotional abuse dished out to both him and his mother. The tears which this brought with his retelling were unexpected, since he had voiced these memories a few times in the past: in a clinical setting and with other "working girls", and even when drunk to complete strangers. In an odd way, it helped to be with someone unlikely to care; he hadn't forgot he was paying for Claire's time. Only with someone you know and trust can you be truly hurt. That was another of the things life had taught him.

She sat back in the room's only chair and drank the over-priced booze as he divulged his innermost thoughts. As he sipped his third glass of whisky, his inhibitions began to loosen, freeing up his tongue and the depth of his recollections. The more he drank, the more important it became to share his memories with another human being, perhaps in the hope the act of sharing could stem their influence on his weary mind.

At around one, he finished. Tears were in his eyes, but Claire simply shrugged and said, "You've been through the mill then."

It was obvious she didn't care, but then why should she? He couldn't condemn her. He was equally guilty of not caring and so he shrugged as well. *Fair enough*, he thought.

Reaching for his wallet, he counted out close to a hundred pounds, passed it to her and said, "Let's call it half a night. You should be able to get a taxi from reception."

She made for the door but paused while holding it half open. "You should find yourself some help before you do something drastic."

Michael nodded and the door closed behind her on a cold whisper of air. He was alone. Things had become heavy over the course of the night but, despite a wealth of disclosure on his part, his memories still haunted him. Try as he might, he couldn't shake them off and so he sought to combat his demons by emptying the mini bar, stretching out on his bed and, with the room spinning once again, falling asleep.

Fifteen

Finding himself back in a recurring dream, Michael dreamt about the night after their return from Blackpool. Michael and his mother found themselves alone on the back porch while his father had fallen asleep and was now snoring to himself in an armchair. The mere presence of his mother — as long as his father was absent — satisfied his need for nurturing. Away from the teasing of his peers, the abuse from his headmaster and the domination of his father, no words were needed. Only she accepted him fully, never bullied him and hardly ever even chastised him. With her, he felt calm. They were both introverts, slow to express things, especially emotions. They didn't talk about the way their patriarch behaved towards them. But that did not matter; words were cheaper than actions. His mother would stroke his hair and hold him in a loose embrace. That was what mattered. The quiet times with his mother were complemented by his being alone in his daydream world.

His father's extrovert style was in marked contrast to that of Michael and his mother. His father was impatient, outspoken, always on the verge of hitting out, though, unlike a typical authoritarian figure, he ignored social hierarchy. Yet the way he scapegoated his closest family members suggested he regarded them as inferior. *Is he just a sadist?* Michael wondered. His behaviour did conform to Freud's notion of "displacement" as Michael understood it from his reading. Michael had started to appreciate this philosophical opposite to his father's knee-jerk reactions as it involved careful non-emotive consideration whilst questioning the reasons and motivations behind such phenomena and behaviour.

He found himself compelled to wonder why something was happening, including the things his father did. His patience and tolerance, both modelled by his mother and possibly inherited from her as well, led him to treat others well. And yet there were two areas in which he fell short. Despite attempting to understand what made his father tick, he had not reached the perfect plateau of forgiving and forgetting; he still felt hurt, bitter and disappointed. And secondly, although he had avoided turning into his father, he knew he had the same potential to have been — or to become — an arsehole just like him. Michael did also have a streak of sadism. It was there at the backyard stream, above a trout's writhing body. Life and death. Power. He hoped, however, that the feeling of remorse he felt after these fishing episodes made him a different person with the potential to make different choices.

He awoke with a hangover. He was so used to them now that they were losing their edge, but today there were additional symptoms: a pounding head, exhaustion, depression. He thought of it as his body wreaking its revenge for excess. He could seek help, as Claire had suggested, but saw no point. He was heading on a downwards spiral anyway.

First though, a shower, brushed teeth and a change of clothes. Where would he go today? East? Past Edinburgh, then further north towards St Andrews? Further away from it all? That might halt the spiral. Satchel packed, bill paid and soon behind the wheel, travelling east.

A few hours of nobody's company but his own now awaited him. Maybe he'd pick up a hitchhiker as he had with Lisa just a few days ago. However, what he needed right now wasn't the false melodrama of company but some strong black coffee to help sober him up. For the third time in a week, he probably had too much alcohol in his system to be driving so instead of waiting for a rest stop, he soon pulled over to the hard shoulder where a small mobile roadside cafe was situated. He got himself two large coffees with milk and no sugar.

"Rough night?" the proprietor asked, noticing his bloodshot eyes and general shabbiness.

Michael paid up and walked away from him in silence. He put both coffees carefully on the passenger seat as he lit another cigarette and waited for the drinks to cool. A police car passed by and, while he crossed his fingers it continued without slowing, he took his keys from out of the ignition and started on his coffee, swallowing deep as it was now cool enough to drink without the risk of scalding his mouth.

Twenty minutes later, he felt vaguely human again, but he wasn't ready to leave just yet as the sight of the passing police car had left him shaken. Eventually hunger got the better of him, but, as he just didn't trust the food at mobile cafes, he started the car and pulled out into the middle lane, making sure he obeyed the speed limit.

Despite the pangs in his stomach, he decided to keep driving further north. Any hitchhikers would be out of luck because, following his short interaction with Lisa, he had — somewhere in the deep recesses of his mind — reached an epiphany. Realising life was tenuous and fleeting, he didn't feel like chancing any further introverted thoughts, whether conscious or otherwise, with another hitchhiker looking for a free ride. Michael pressed down hard on the accelerator and allowed his mind to wander; soon "daydreaming" and reminiscing once again.

Sixteen

Following an unusually late dinner, his father had fallen asleep in an armchair in a corner of the parlour. His mother, seizing this rare opportunity, had followed Michael out to the untamed rear lawn which was alive with the sounds of bats and night-birds and the meandering stream. An American-style porch bench swung gently in the breeze as dew fell. They sat under a full moon; the house behind them and the grounds bathed in surreal grey light. In silence, his mother pulled him close and stroked his hair affectionately.

He breathed in deeply.

Nothing seemed to stir but Michael knew their little patch of land was alive with all sorts of wildlife: down by the riverbank, trout and midges; over towards the meadow, owls and mice; closest to them, spiders waited patiently with a hunter's instinct for any unfortunate insect to snag itself inside their painstaking webs. All of them driven by the fight for survival. Rocking back and forth on the back porch, mother and son too were in the same battle. Unlike the wild creatures though, Michael faced the additional challenge of a crippling self-consciousness. He felt as though he was watching the set of a battle scene, filmed from above, and with the director saving his comments for later. Their own predator slept indoors, oblivious.

From above, they looked to be a perfect pair, hunched together in the dusk. However, his mother's faith set her apart from Michael. For him, biblical stories were fairy tales. Justice. Retribution. Punishment. The promise of Heaven, the threat of Hell. Sinners or the saved. Purgatory, limbo, immortality through consciousness surviving death. These were biologically impossible concepts, Michael knew. He had his five senses; all the rest was bullshit.

It was a shame he could not express the way he had come to these conclusions; could not share with his mother, the only person he most trusted, his maturing individuality. But he just didn't want to court her disappointment. Although he did have some use for the big themes of the Old Testament after all: hatred, for example, and vengeance. Indeed, right now, he was imagining forcing his father's head into the river, holding him down with a strength he didn't possess. Watching as the last pockets of air escaped from his mouth and broke the water's surface. It gave him pleasure, which was another thing he felt compelled to keep a secret.

Deep thoughts, he mused as he kicked out at the ground beneath the bench. After an hour or so, his father woke from his slumber. As he roused, Michael's mother hurried indoors in time to settle down in a swivel corner chair situated across from his dad's lounger. She'd timed it too late though. As Michael peered through the Venetian blinds of the living room window, his dad stood and, in a single movement, struck her in the face whilst shouting a familiar slur. Michael attempted to block out his fear and the familiar feeling of impotence. He focused on the babble of the stream to distract him from the shouts and screams, but soon he was covering his ears with the palms of his hands to escape the harsh reality he was so sadly used to.

Seventeen

St Andrews was quiet at quarter to two and Michael parked in a district of the town facing the North Sea. The road was brimful of bars. Streamers and party poppers lined the tarmac; the remnants of some hen or stag party. They blew gently in the breeze. He kicked them out of his way as he strode along the shoreline as a light rain drizzled down. Stopping at the pier, he leant over its balustrade and took in a deep breath. A long drop from the pier would solve all of his problems permanently. But he could have done that back at Blackpool so, exhaling, he turned around and retraced his footsteps.

There were a few guest houses facing the road and pier. Selecting one at random, he went in, straightening up his shirt and trousers. After ringing the service bell, a portly looking woman greeted him and he asked for a room. He was soon slumping down on the bed, having again paid in advance — this time for three days. He would hit the bars later, but in the meantime, he decided to nap for a few hours. He closed his eyes and slept.

Eighteen

He slept and, for a change, it wasn't alcohol-induced. He saw things vividly as a dream played itself out.

He stood in a corridor of the old school after setting the building alight. Things were dark and, while he squinted, raindrops slammed against the windows. A fierce storm rocked the building and wind seemed on the verge of smashing its way inside. Michael prayed it would. Anything to redirect the fear which he now felt.

He walked forwards as slowly as he could wanting only to cover his ears with his hands. Smoke soon surrounded him though and the heat from the fire made him sweat. The surge of adrenaline caused his heart to beat wildly, but still he continued to stride towards the source. He felt helpless and vulnerable, but also curious to witness the conflagration which was in the process of wiping out the entire schoolhouse. He seemed to be just an observer here though and breathing in the smoke-filled air and feeling the heat did little to slow his progress. *Curiosity killed the cat*, he thought as he continued towards the old classrooms, coughing fiercely as the smoke caught the back of his throat. Soon he was sneezing while his eyes watered, and his vision slowly cleared as the fire and smoke did likewise.

He began to feel relief, but the sensation was replaced by elation when he heard the spitting sound of the burning wood. Eventually, he collapsed onto the non-existent floor as his dreamscape altered and shifted. He found himself walking down the old corridor which he feared more than every punishment he'd ever been subjected to. The deafening sound of silence now pierced his ears, and he wished the fire would catch hold in this part of the old building while he watched. Pleased with his actions, which he felt — on some level at least — were fully justified, he couldn't wipe the smile from his face. He found the exit door, which on any other occasion had served to empty the west wing of its screaming occupants at the beginning of every break and at the end of each school day. The continuous sound of splitting wooden door frames, coat hooks, hangers and the plethora of assorted combustibles reached his ears. It was an utterly welcome noise and a further boost to his feeling of elation.

Now totally immersed inside his dreamland, Michael pushed his way through the oak exit doors of the west wing and gasped in the pure clear air which replaced the deadly smoke billowing from every section of the building. Coughing harshly, he managed to clear his chest, and he recollected the sights, smells and sounds as he watched from the safety of the schoolyard perimeter. As before, he sensed a deep feeling of elation. The wind suddenly changed direction, moving southwards, and all too quickly his mouth and nostrils were again filled with the sensation of burning wood, seared metal and slate. The air around him also carried the sound of broken timbers falling onto the scorched earth.

What he'd instigated was criminal, but again he questioned whether he was owed this jaunt into the world of arson. Following years of subjugation and mental torture, for him the only cure was to hit back at the institution which had made his suffering possible — and actively encouraged it.

He now decided it was time to leave before the emergency services started to arrive; their shrill and screaming sirens were already intruding on the early morning silence. It would be a crime to him if he was ever caught and prosecuted for his sweet revenge. He walked casually away across the schoolyard and playing fields, making an effort to look like an innocent bystander strolling away from the scene. Meanwhile, once more, a silent scream of elation passed by his lips.

Nineteen

S creams from outside.

Michael had slept for five and a half hours and the pubs and clubs were now opening their doors to the revellers who had swarmed in ready for their weekly dose of fun. From the shadows behind his second-storey window, he stared down at the crowds. He was enjoying seeing how irresponsible and foolish people became under the influence of alcohol or drugs. With that thought in mind, he soon made his decision. Delving into his satchel, he retrieved a scruffy T-shirt. "GLOBAL HYPERCOLOUR" was printed across the front. It was blue, but a night of sweating would turn it to orange and, after he had slipped it on, he put on a pair of faded jeans and laced his trainers.

Like most alcoholics, he had an emergency stash of booze located in the side pocket of his bag. He needed a little Dutch courage so he drank deeply, letting the

Scotch tingle his throat. Normally, Michael would avoid crowds but tonight he wanted something stronger than drink: if you knew where to find them, a rave or a club were the best sources for a range of drugs.

He reminded himself that Lisa's young life was likely blighted by drugs. And, apart from the drink, he'd been chemical-free for more than a decade. Yet recent events had made him wish for the past emotions of his "drug phase". He was conflicted by an empathy towards other addicts and a sense of shame regarding his own struggles. He had become depressed after his discussion with Lisa and his fleeting but intense interaction with Claire. Michael always attempted not to let negative life experiences affect him. He even felt he was becoming an expert on the subject, although his own negativity, caused by negative experience, had left him bitter. The absence of concern — on the part of other people and whatever God one might turn to — was the source of this resentment. Indifference was prevalent, and it did offer an easy way out, but for Michael, a life without affection and empathy was a wasted one. He supposed the love his mother had lavished on him in boyhood had saved him from becoming selfish, cynical, sadistic and violent, like his father.

He allowed these thoughts to dissipate as he began to focus on his latest mission: the acquisition of his first "hit" for a decade. He was streetwise enough to get what he wanted and today he even looked the part. Police sniffer dogs were the main worry, but Michael had no intention of risking crossing their paths near the clubs and so decided he would ask further afield. Sitting on his bed, he drank and drank until he felt confident enough to leave and within half an hour, the alcohol in his system had reached his head.

He strode out of the door, locking it behind him and found what he was looking for next to his car. A group of people had gathered around it and he offered one of them a ride. But luck wasn't going his way as, half a mile outside of town, he was forced to exchange a tenner for a small wrap of speed when he was really hoping for cocaine. Placing a small amount on his tongue, he taste-tested it and felt sure it was kosher.

Deciding to leave the car away from the pier, he walked back to the guest house with his new "friend" in tow. His name was Mark and he was soon inviting Michael to a party. He declined and headed back to his room where he twisted the speed up into a ball, placed it into his mouth and swallowed it with a gulp of Scotch. A few moments later, his heart was thudding in his chest. His mouth was dry, his breathing fierce and his thoughts were racing. He lay on the bed while the clamour inside him was joined by the thud-thud of a baseline tearing out from near the pier. The screech of souped-up cars passed back and forth along the roadway.

Perched on the edge of his bed, he drank and drank. Eventually, Michael undressed and took another shower in the room's claustrophobic ensuite. Tepid water drenched his body while, little by little, the speed — but not the alcohol — left his system and his heart's manic beating subsided. Then he dried himself with the bathroom's only towel and lay down on the bed.

He wanted to sleep but the nap he'd taken earlier and the speed were mitigating against it, so, at around midnight, he dressed himself again and left his room in search of a downer. First, he wanted to check on his car and he hoped the walk itself would also help clear his head. Swaying a little, he crisscrossed the crowds until he had passed by the pier and then carried on walking for a quarter of a mile. Back at the car, he discovered it had been keyed. It was only a few scratches, but it was enough to seriously piss him off.

"Bastard," Michael shouted as he unlocked his Celica and sat in the driver's seat; the sounds from the pier still ringing in his ears. Anger made adrenaline coarse through him.

He'd known it would happen to such an expensive car sooner or later though. Up to now, he conceded, he'd been lucky. He'd had the Celica for a decade or more, but this possibility had been in the back of his mind from the moment he'd driven out of the showroom carpark.

"Call it karma," he consoled himself.

And yet, although he knew the car was inanimate and despite the many counselling sessions he'd attended in which he had been encouraged to put random events into perspective, Michael couldn't help viewing the keying as an attack on himself. His T-shirt was drenched. He was an alcoholic, with no meaningful relationships, work or home. The speed had left him wrung out after the initial mania. He was in a rut, drifting, both physically and mentally. His thoughts wandered to the secret he kept hidden. Swaddled in a blanket under the back seat was a military-issue revolver, fully loaded and brought back by his paternal grandfather from the Great War.

He'd been lucky not to have been stopped by the police in Glasgow; possession of a loaded handgun would land him in jail for a quite considerable time, even though now the only danger was to him alone. In other dark and depressing moments such as this one, he'd loaded it with just one bullet, spun the cylinder and played a game of Russian roulette with himself. He'd done it twice before this road trip, but death hadn't come knocking. His luck, however, was a torture in itself and for a while he got to thinking about how harshly the world had treated him, past and present.

With that thought, Michael reached behind him and, throwing the blanket aside, clasped hold of the gun.

Popping open the cylinder, he checked all six bullets were in place. He put the barrel to his right temple and placed his index finger on the trigger. Sweat ran down from his forehead and, as it reached his cheek, he lowered the gun and pressed down lightly on its safety catch. Just one more square inch of pressure would have been enough.

It was a sobering thought.

Michael put the gun into the glovebox, locking it up out of harm's way. He hoped to hell no car thieves found it. Therefore, he decided the car would be less at risk in its previous spot so drove it back. The clubs and pubs had shut their doors now and only a few stragglers remained at the pier, a little worse for wear after their night's jubilations. They called over to him as he reached the guest house door, probably looking for a dry place to continue their night's antics. Ignoring them, he began to feel safer. Not only from strangers but also from himself. The pistol was in the glovebox, the car was secure, and his bed awaited.

PART TWO

Twenty

Michael stared out of the window where he could see the turbulence of the sea and the waves crashing all along St Andrews' promenade. He had moved to a Travelodge on the other side of the town and, after the better part of a week of sobriety following the third attempt on his life, he found himself wondering what in the hell had happened to him? Why had he just turned the tables on a decade's worth of sobriety? Was it stress, self-destruction? Or just plain hedonism?

The town was also inhabited by a soulless, snoopy and unenlightened bunch of people from whom Michael felt alienated. So, why stay?

Ignoring this question, he decided on a dose of fresh air — lighting up yet another cigarette on his way — and walked the few yards to the promenade. He was alone, yet this suited him fine. Only the sound of crashing waves cut through the silence, and he allowed his mind to drift. However, his head was soon filled with unwelcome thoughts of the abusive relationship he had had with his now dead father. He would have preferred the relative silence of the external world of the present, but something deep inside insisted on taking him back there so, drowning out the sound of the waves, he allowed a series of memories to take command of his own jaded internal arena.

On the tail-end of a summer's afternoon, Michael found himself crossing the weed-strewn yard at the back of the home he shared with his mother and father. His dad had left some time earlier and yet, unfortunately for him, Michael soon heard the front door open and then slam shut with the usual force typical of his father after a drunken binge. Usually, it was his mother who bore the brunt of his fury but being overdue a beating from his father for a poor performance on his latest home schooling task, Michael knew, almost absolutely, that today he would be the primary target.

He was soon proven right as his father approached him at speed, dragging him by his arm directly into his study. For a while, the pain in his arm stripped away the fear, but within moments, it was replaced by a stinging in his hands as his dad applied the frayed cane which he always kept handy in the corner of his study.

Things were always more draining when his father was the punisher because, even though the level of pain was similar to that inflicted by his headmaster, things were much more personal when it was his dad dealing out the abuse. In addition to the physical pain, Michael felt a degree of betrayal as he continued to view his father as some sort of role model. The pain wasn't just physical but was also emotionally damaging because, with each rare attempt at some sort of paternal guidance, Michael — even now with his hands seeping blood — on some deep, dark level felt disappointment more than pain.

Michael knew, despite the severity of the pain he was inflicting on his son, his dad was enjoying the experience. Maybe it was in the flood of adrenaline and an unhealthy dose of testosterone where he got his kicks. After all, with his dad's selfish outlook, there had to be something in it for him.

Michael continued to endure the brunt of his father's rage until on one of the final strokes, he caught hold of the tip of the cane and wrenched it from his father's hand. He knew what would follow but through his tears, he saw something in his dad's cobalt blue eyes that was deader than usual. If he'd swallowed his mother's preachings, Michael would have sworn that what he was seeing was pure uninhibited evil and yet, despite his reticence, he also sensed a soul drained of empathy. Even as his dad switched his tool of torture to a studded belt, Michael uttered a silent prayer for his father's soul.

That had been the first and only time in which he had stood up to his dad, at least physically. He had challenged his father's behaviour on many occasions deep inside his own head where imagination had become a useful ally on innumerable jaunts into the fantastical movie set of his mind. And so, following a good lashing from the belt, his dad left him weeping in a corner of the study where, as usual, Michael felt the deep need for his mother's embraces and soft words.

Back in the present, however, Michael, stuck staring out across the North Sea on a damp and weather-beaten bench, looked over his shoulder with some longing at the entrance to the nearest pub.

It was now one o'clock in the afternoon, and he had been trying to avoid drinking all morning. He wasn't looking for company at this hour, and he doubted he'd find it. Indeed, after negotiating the short walk to the entrance, he found the pub was completely empty. He ordered up a pint and, halfway through, decided he was hungry. He was soon stuffing his face with eggs, chips and beans followed by an ice cream which made his teeth ache.

Leaving a generous tip, he headed for the door but changed his mind when he saw rain hammering down outside. The entrance to the lodge and his room were only a few short steps away but the rain was enough of an excuse to stay tucked away inside the pub. He was lying to himself again but brushed it off as the barman poured him pint number three. *That will be it*, he told himself. It wasn't. He got falling-over drunk and only just made it back to his room without injury.

The rest of the day was a blur until about ten that night when he found himself leaving the lodge. Feeling only slightly sober, he strolled towards the pier and sat himself on the same low bench. There he stayed, smoking the last of his cigarettes while his mind drifted on waves of recollection. Finding himself slipping away from the present once more, he was soon reminiscing. This time pondering his own shortcomings.

It had been a good quarter-century since he'd left his school days behind and yet little seemed to have changed. The same nagging thought processes were still at play inside his head and so, back in the present, he actively attempted to counter these depressing, self-destructive thoughts by retrieving a penknife from his jacket pocket. He placed the blade into the palm of his left hand and cut through the skin. A crimson trickle ran between his fingers and spattered onto the ground, soon diverting these malign and intrusive mental reflections. He felt no pain but knew it would sting like hell later. However, this wasn't just self-harm. He had taken an oath to himself and as he left the deserted pier, he wrapped his bleeding hand in a handkerchief and made his way back to his car, spilling blood onto the ground all the way.

Blood — the crimson, viscous trickle — was familiar. Although he only occasionally indulged in self-harm through cutting, the beatings he had received during his life were countless. Physical pain and, in particular, the visual evidence of hurt that blood displayed had been easier to handle than the chronic emotional bullying of his school cohorts. Peer pressure might work as a guide to behaviour in simple societies, he felt, but unless individuals who struggled with social behaviour were guided with respect and affection, it became derision and then rejection as punishment for non-conformity. Free will and maturity were hard won.

Later, when he was older, Michael had considered that he and his peers had been on autopilot while they waited, through adolescence and puberty, for adulthood to open their eyes and enable them to strive for what Maslow had termed "self-actualisation". Meantime, the simple seesawing of pain and pleasure kept a person going on a carnival ride of emotion both positive and negative in nature. Right now, the negative, in his throbbing palm, outweighed the positive. The flow of blood would cease but he knew the pain would hang around for days, if not weeks. It was a good deflection for him but it also came along with the added problem of explaining the wound to those curious and nosy enough to enquire. But at that moment, he cared very little. All he wanted to do was get back to his car.

There, he doused his wound in antiseptic and did his best to dress it with a bandage from the first aid kit. He wrapped it around his left hand after first soaking it in surgical spirits. Then he found himself retrieving his revolver from the glovebox. With his injured hand in the left side pocket of his jacket and the gun in his right, he walked the few yards to the reception area of the lodge. Taking the stairs up to his room, he unlocked the door, lay on the bed and stared at the ceiling. There he stayed until, realising that sleep wouldn't come, he got up, went over to the window and stared out over the half-empty parking lot. Rain continued to fall from the heavens but he felt trapped. All he had for company was his own thoughts and they could be as dangerous as the gun in his pocket.

The pubs were shut. He had no booze and the phrase "bouncing off the walls" felt apt. Staring out of the window, Michael found himself helplessly ruminating whilst the double-glazed barrier protected him from an intense spell of wind and rain. For a while, the view from his window seemed picturesque and St Andrews' picture-postcard landscape lifted his mood. Feelings of safety and security caused him to reflect on his early life before everything had turned sour and so Michael found himself drawing forth the more pleasant emotions associated with his very early childhood and then again later, following his father's sweet departure from the family home.

The love he had received from his mother had greatly outweighed the indifference his father displayed towards him. Instead of bonding with his son during the boy's younger years, Michael's father often dismissed him. Something he hadn't at that tender age realised was preferable to the kind of attention his father would display towards him later. Despite the indifference Michael began to show to his father shortly after his departure, his dad, stubbornly, had attempted to keep a grip on his son through distorting the truth.

However, the contents of most of the letters sent to him had remained unopened whilst the rest of them had been only partially read by Michael and then promptly burnt. He could have just binned them but there had been a symbolic satisfaction in burning which, with any other form of disposal, could never be achieved.

As he stared out of his window on a dark and stormy night, these thoughts made him grin from ear-to-ear and even prompted a few chuckles. Eventually, these chuckles transformed into full-fledged laughter, fading his craving for a drink just as the air exiting his lungs fogged-up the double-glazed divide protecting him from the intensity of the storm. Under the sodium-orange glow of the streetlights, details of the scene outside began to blur as happy tears began to flow.

His father's departure had granted him something money couldn't buy: the freedom to think, feel and act as he wished. For the first time in his life, he felt he had as much autonomy as others in his peer group while also knowing he could still rely on the complete emotional access and support of the sweetest, kindest, most forgiving woman he had ever known: his mother.

Drying his eyes with the backs of his hands, Michael assured himself that no one cared but himself and so he let the tears well up as they would. He was happy just to sit and stare out of the window as the southerly gusts collided with this thin barrier and he was soon basking in memories of his mother's loose embraces, which would carry on well into his young adulthood. That the length of intense maternal support had been extended was not a source of embarrassment to him; his father's prohibitions had previously prevented his mother from expressing consistent support so maybe he'd been well overdue for some sort of catchup.

Back in the present, his hangovers and moodiness were pushed to the back of his mind while happy tears continued to flow. These tears offered a glimpse of hope between the despondence of his present and the complete uncertainty of his future.

Exhausted, he surrounded himself with loving memories and lay fully clothed on the bed. He shut his eyes and drifted off.

Twenty-One

The clock fixed to the desk read quarter to twelve. Michael calculated he'd slept his way through a good eight hours. He was now faced with an afternoon and night with not a thing to do. He needed something to stimulate him and so, after taking a shower and changing his clothes, he left the lodge and went out to his car.

A few miles on, he pulled into the carpark of a local loch and made his way to a pub which stood on the south bank. Once installed in the beer garden of The Red Lion, he sat staring out across the scenery. The view was beautiful. He supped at his beer and let his mind drift. There he remained, two pints and an hour and a half later.

The pub was deserted, and he'd avoided the bartender by sitting outside. He smoked his way through a pack of ten and was about to cross the road to a small shop when he paused to take in the serenity of the place.

The scene had started to lift his mood and so he went back inside the pub, bought a packet of cigarettes from the machine next to a faded pool table and got himself a half-pint of orange juice from the bar.

"Enjoying the view?" the bartender asked.

Michael smiled. He'd make a move shortly — two pints and an orange juice were enough for him — but he didn't feel like heading back just yet. Still smiling, he decided on a little detour on his way back to the Travelodge and found himself on the eastern side of the loch, walking across hills and dirt-covered pathways until he stopped at a wooden jetty. He watched as several anglers cast their lines out onto the choppy surface of the loch but it wasn't ideal fishing weather.

Under his father's instruction, he'd learnt how to handle a rod on similar lakes back home in Wales, even managing to catch a few sizeable pike, perch and carp. Back in the present though, there was a chill in the air and the wind blew harshly but the anglers, mostly elderly men, seemed content enough with their time alone away from their humdrum lives and wives in the suburbs.

But the fishing scene brought back the harsh memory of that undeserved slap on a deserted beach in Blackpool. Still watching the men, Michael continued around the loch, attracting nods and hellos as he passed. Sometimes he'd stop and inquire as to their luck, or lack of it. But all the while, his mind was really on autopilot. His thoughts produced a negative state of mind. He remembered not just the slap he'd received — he'd been well used to those — but rather the menace and malice on his father's face. A dark cloud lowered. The weather at the loch remained unchanged but he now started to wonder how cold the water would be if he found the courage to jump in.

An overhanging cleft separated him from the loch and, for a while, he stood at its edge, staring down at the turbulent shore while flirting with the idea of suicide. For a while it was his only thought, but before long he found himself hitting the surface of the water. The temperature rendered him impotent. Hypothermia kicked in as his nervous system began to shut down. He slipped deeper into the dark depths as his brain began to be starved of precious oxygen. Then, he began to feel a not unpleasant rush. Time began to lose meaning as he descended into the oblivion of freezing loch water and the all-encompassing pitch blackness gave way to yet another sunny day in June.

Instead of making the most of the sunshine outside, Michael sat rigidly in a chair in his father's study where he relished, not just the gentle breeze from the room's free-standing fan, but also the steady hypnotic sound of his father's voice. He could hear the words, but he focused primarily on the pitch. Each word accentuated by the deep and rich Welsh accent composed and considered with every breath he took.

Lethargy kicked in. A mood which later could earn him another beating. But now he was glad to just drift off while precious circuits in his mind began, slowly and inevitably, to shut themselves down.

Unwelcome hands grasped him from above; shouts, panicked and concerned.

Back on land, he shivered and vomited up lake water in front of the small crowd gathered round him. Still outside his body and time, Michael's mind stayed underwater, lost in memories. Some touched on his dad's rare attempts at paternal bonding, but these recollections soon turned sour as his dad's low-pitched voice droned on. Michael then found himself doubled over the desk while his father uttered words of chastisement and anger. The wooden cane, fetched from its place in the corner, put to violent use across the small of Michael's back. And back to the lake shore. Vomiting again, he shook violently as paramedics wrapped him in thermal blankets and managed to slow down his breathing.

At the hospital, Michael told the medics he'd slipped on sodden grass and panicked. He got the distinct impression they were dubious though and so he proceeded, convincingly he thought, to lie his way through their doubts. Fortunately, his previous suicidal thoughts on two separate piers had led to nothing, otherwise he was sure they would have sectioned him for his own safety. As his body recovered from a severe case of hypothermia, he pronounced himself "tip-top" as he stared into the bloodshot eyes of his designated physician. He turned out to be a junior doctor fresh out of training and Michael guessed him to be over-worked and sleep deprived. He was soon questioning Michael on his lifestyle, droning on about drink, drugs and his addiction to smoking.

As this quack seemed curt and short-tempered, Michael stood his ground on all three counts while, deep inside, maintaining his vices were his business alone.

This switch in questioning to his state of mind frustrated him more, but Michael gave nothing away beyond a deadpan look as the doctor prattled on about healthy living. This doctor had got him down to a tee, but Michael ignored such portents of premature death by nodding feigned agreement as he let this well-rehearsed speech wash over him, pretending to listen, understand and comprehend the "damage" he was doing to his body.

He acted it all out perfectly and, following a single night of observation, he was discharged with no more fucking lectures and just a strip of blue pills to combat the shock which he just didn't seem to feel.

Twenty-Two

The following morning, Michael left the hospital with a strange sense of renewal that stayed with him as he took a taxi back to the loch to pick up his car.

He prepared to leave what might have been the scene of his own death and, for a time, he felt remorseful. His mother had often told him suicide was a selfish, sinful act. She'd helped him learn and recite passages of scripture, but he'd failed, or refused, to understand those verses. Sitting on a rickety chair in the parlour, she tried to give him a moral steer with her comforting, soft-accented words. Now, as then, empathy connected them far deeper than love. He knew no one as caring and considerate, yet this was the source of his father's criticism. Might others also seek to shame her for the level of her tolerance? In the face of those who sought to victimise her, she either would not or could not retaliate: physically, verbally, through action or through mental means, such as freezing out, sulking or disapproval. She had no interest in evening the score, either on her own behalf or that of others, including Michael himself.

Only half listening but still taking in the scripture verses, Michael allowed his mind to drift to times when she'd tried to nurse him while his father had been boozing at the pub, fishing in the river, or, in Michael's younger years, reading in his library. Fishing and reading had become valued pastimes of his own. Later, however, the vice and pleasure inherent in heavy drinking he'd discover all by himself. His mother was all but teetotal; hardly ever touching the demon booze. Her only vice was smoking: a habit that would, later in her life, become her undoing. However, these unwelcome memories returned him to the present day and he found himself staring out across the loch on a damp and dreary morning. However, today, it seemed most of the fishermen had chosen to stay indoors as most of the jetties were deserted.

For a while, he bathed in the relative silence. Then he lit a cigarette, ignoring his doctor's advice. The little pep talk had irritated him and so, in defiance, he leant back on the bonnet of his car to enjoy his smoke whilst it flooded his system with carcinogens; all the while doing his utmost not to dwell on his antics of the previous day.

Unfortunately, he was soon recognised by one of the few anglers who happened to be in the process of packing up his fishing gear into the boot of an old Volkswagen Beetle. For a while, Michael thought him dismissive until he waved in his general direction and, despite Michael's lack of response, was soon crossing the space between them both. Michael recognised him as one of his rescuers and, as he came towards him, he spoke.

"Michael, isn't it?" he asked.

Michael nodded. "Wales' answer to Jacques Cousteau." For a second, Michael grasped for a name. He'd been out of it during his drowning episode and so couldn't be quite sure of the man's name, but Roy seemed to fit.

"I noticed your accent yesterday," Roy said. "I suspected that you were far from home."

"Just a couple of hundred miles."

Roy smiled and asked, "How are you now? Any better?"

Looking across the loch once more, Michael considered his answer. It was obvious to them both that Roy meant his mind as well as his body, but Michael said, "Not bad. Suffice to say that I prefer indoor swimming now."

Smiling, Roy offered him his hand and re-introduced himself, adding a surname which was not in the least bit Scottish. "Pritchard, Roy Pritchard."

Michael was taken aback, Pritchard being a relatively common Welsh surname, alongside his own — top of the list — name of Jones.

Roy added, "I've Welsh blood in me too but I've never been there."

Michael smiled back. "Postcards don't do it justice."

"I'm sure they don't," he responded. "You here on business or pleasure?"

"A bit of both really."

Michael continued to exchange words with the man for a couple of minutes more before succumbing to disinterest and the frigid air circulating around the loch and its relatively small carpark.

Roy wished him goodbye, adding a poignant "Good luck" before crossing back over to the Beetle. Strangely, Michael found himself lifted by the interaction despite his reticence. Conversing with this stranger had put a smile on his face and as he set off back to his room, it remained.

Getting back to the lodge, he was relieved he'd hung a "do not disturb" sign on the door handle before he'd left. He still had his gun and ammo under his pillows. If discovered, the police would likely have been alerted along with their armed response unit. He thanked God he hadn't stayed away any longer as he had only paid for a week's stay. The gun and ammo lay exactly where he'd left them and as he reloaded, slipped on the safety catch and placed it into his satchel, he realised he'd acquired a new form of cowardice.

The pub awaited him for his evening "night cap" and so, after a quick shower and shave, he left, carefully locking his satchel first.

At the bar, he was served vodka and tonics by a harassed-looking bartender. As usual, Michael avoided conversation. He was the only customer in the place, and surprised himself by thinking of very little, remaining focused on nothing but the bar, the simple act of standing and binge-drinking. However, after a while his trance-like state gave way to a series of boredom-induced recollections.

Twenty-Three

Michael, now in his early teens, was hard at work in his father's study, re-reading Orwell's *1984*. It was close to two o'clock and he'd been sitting in the same chair for hours. He leant forwards slightly to avoid scraping the tender parts of his lower back. Despite it being almost a week since his beating and even though the pain had morphed into mere discomfort, Michael couldn't seem to shake off the memory of that afternoon. It had started to affect his attention span.

After he had wrenched the cane from his dad's hand, the remainder of the beating had been extremely violent, lasting a full five minutes. Michael had stayed doubled-over his father's desk, enduring stroke after stroke from, firstly, the frayed cane but then also from the metal-studded belt.

The beating had come from Michael's failure to correctly answer certain questions his father had asked about the novel — at least initially — before the additional punishment that followed his wrenching the cane out of his father's hand. Afterwards, Michael realised the thrust of the questions had gone over his father's head as they referred to psychological concepts which he despised. Even at the age he was then, Michael recognised the parallels between his dad's overbearing behaviour and the all-seeing, all-knowing Big Brother. He saw himself as the captive of a cruel regime. Repercussions would have ensued had he ventured such opinions, so in this second visit to the room to study *1984*, he re-read avidly, keeping his eyes fixed on each page — apart from surreptitious glances at the clock.

When the clock struck four, Michael heard the purposeful stride of his father approaching him. His footsteps, echoing throughout the hallway and study, stopped directly behind him. Michael could feel his dad leaning over his left shoulder, peering for a second or two at the open pages. He snatched at the paperback. Michael could hear him breathing as he read through the section for himself. Marking it with a bookmark, he set the paperback down, and asked, "What have you learnt?"

His first thought was *do not disappoint Father*. Instead, Michael told him all he thought he wanted to hear. At first, he seemed satisfied. Michael had spared himself a beating by the skin of his teeth by understanding enough of the book to successfully placate his father.

Having then been dismissed, he went outside to the yard once again and tried to ignore the emotional pain the insight into his father's character always brought. Soon, the sun started going down. Childish fantasies had taken him on a magical journey aboard pirate ships, wartime destroyers and frigates for the past few hours, but the shadows of the house and its grounds were fast increasing in their length and breadth. At close to marching pace, he returned through reeds and shrubs to the house.

Inside, all was still and quiet beyond the faint hum of a few fans keeping the house cool. For a while, Michael stood at the back entrance leading into the kitchen. Drumming up the courage to step inside, a heavy sheen of sweat had broken out on his forehead whilst ahead of him, the kitchen's wall clock was counting down the seconds to seven: his curfew hour.

He'd returned just in the nick of time. The steady clunk of his father's footsteps on the slate floor now resounded throughout the ground level. Michael felt his heartbeat increase as he appeared from his study and gave him an almost disappointed look. While he was scared by the frown and would remember it, it would be the memory of that disappointment that Michael would relish for days to come because rebellion could be practised and displayed in many different ways.

Twenty-Four

A few short months since his suicidal attempt at the loch, Michael found himself slumped on a cold concrete floor; his legs stretched out as he finished a joint. Overhead, an array of colours lit up the night sky as fireworks rocketed high above him. The noise he didn't like, but the spectrum of colour was attractive. For a while, he regretted that he hadn't joined the celebrations but even in a room full of people, he'd still be alone. He would rather be *completely* alone, free from any pretence.

His head span as he stood upright. The remnants of the evening's jubilations surrounded him. The remains of bottle rockets, streamers and sparklers carpeted the space where he now stood and for a moment or two, he found himself thinking about his old schoolhouse.

Built near the turn of the century, it had dominated the view from the nearby high street and several of the lanes which cut through the centre of the town. Back then, it had served as both a primary and a secondary school. At the time of the school's construction, the town had been just a small village, but it had since morphed into a rather large township. During the last decade or two, however, the old schoolhouse had become redundant thanks to the building of a modern, contemporary school which had, due to a veritable population explosion, been extended with outside huts due to the lack of available classrooms.

A total of four factors had been responsible for the old schoolhouse's redundancy. The first being the need to accommodate the population increase. Secondly, the place had been full of damp and asbestos, and thirdly it had been badly neglected thanks to funding cuts leading to the loss of a full-time caretaker.

Reason number four?

That was a dark memory and Michael decided not to consider it for more than a fleeting second.

Time to leave, he thought as he brushed himself down.

Home was now a B&B situated on the same open stretch of seafront as the Travelodge. He'd been there, in that same shoddy room, for the better part of three months, often feeling hemmed-in, claustrophobic and restless. At times though, the sheer beauty of the town and landscape brought their own peace and provided him with a level of comfort which just couldn't be bought. With its picture-postcard views and the sound of the crashing waves echoing all along the coastline, the town sometimes instigated feelings of warmth and well-being within him. However, at weekends, it was usually swamped by tourists.

A second wave of fireworks brought him out of his reverie as he began the slow walk home. Passing revellers popped party poppers and wished him a "Happy Hogmanay" on this night where hope for better times prevailed. Despite morose thoughts about how they'd soon be back in the rat race, Michael responded in kind but was glad when he reached his stuffy lodgings. However, whilst unlocking the front door, he noticed lights were on in the living room and kitchen.

He had been invited to his landlady's party and had hoped that by now her guests would have departed, but it now seemed as though half the town was in attendance. He tried slipping past them before he was noticed but it didn't work, and he was soon "mingling" with a glass of cheap champagne, probably Prosecco or Cava, held in his hand. Sitting in a corner of the room, he pretended to be invisible while all the bullshit washed over him. The drunken cacophony soon started to irritate him, so he headed for the back door and the minuscule garden beyond which was packed with half a dozen partygoers. Someone had lit a Catherine Wheel and, as he watched, Michael suddenly felt dizzy at the sight of the spin of colour. Thankfully, it had burnt itself out within thirty seconds and he felt relieved.

He spent another couple of hours standing around, drinking cheap ale out of a dirty glass while longing for his bed where he could sleep off his impending hangover and the weird high gained through the consumption of two powerful intoxicants. Tonight, he had coupled inebriation with cannabis. The latter's mild hallucinogenic effect protecting him from the sensory overload of the early hours of New Year's Day, 1994. Shrugging off people as he headed for the bathroom, he was stopped in his tracks by somebody lightly tapping him on his shoulder.

The woman was in her mid-thirties and very pretty. She reminded him of the major crush of his late childhood: a girl who, through her presence alone, could instigate feelings of excitement and arousal.

Back then, just the thought of her offered a release from a reality of ridicule and physical abuse dealt him by his peers, headmaster or, back at home, by his own father. Even simply catching her reflection in a classroom window, passing her in a school corridor or just by thinking about the shoulder-length strawberry blonde hair which framed her flawless face, would set off movement in his groin. Because he was too young to fully understand, and because his father reacted to everything through a prism of humiliation, he felt embarrassed and ashamed by it.

Thoughts of her would regularly bring about the uncontrollable physical reactions he'd been told by his parents were profoundly sinful. However, Michael soon discovered their opinions were an outdated product of the repressive and depressive attitude of Victorian-era Britain. It was an attitude deeply lodged within his father's philosophical outlook on life and overall mentality, which — had Michael ever dared to challenge — would have risked destroying his father's entire mindset and rendered a further dose of mental or physical abuse inevitable.

Back in the present though, such thoughts evaporated as Michael found himself engaged in a verbal interaction with the woman, instigated only by her asking for directions to the ground floor toilet. He soon realised Helen was as drunk as he was, but before long, they were heading back to her place, just a couple of streets away in an end-of-terrace cottage. The conversation was of love, lust and disappointment. Then she leant towards him, took his hand and led him up the staircase. They made love to the sound of fireworks and fell into a drunken sleep.

Twenty-Five

Following the brutal beating after his short-lived attempt at rebellion, Michael attempted to pay much more attention to the "lessons" provided by his father. But he was a daydreamer, plain and simple. He found his imagination much more stimulating than the real world with its socially-imposed structures that the rebel within him despised. Fantasy came as a welcome relief for him and provided an outlet for the emotions that were denied an arena at home, where his sense of agency was similarly repressed. His social skills were poor, which left him isolated and without allies. At home, as at school, his thoughts and desires went unnoticed, so he lacked any expressive outlet, sense of control over his life and, at times, simple visibility.

All in all, these factors morphed into emotional turmoil. Mostly this manifested itself as anger; a familiar feeling which he directed inwardly instead of beating it down through kicking out or screaming. Instead, he let it fester and it continued to eat away at him. As he grew into adulthood, Michael continued bearing the same highly-charged emotional thought patterns, a burden for which he was completely blameless and one which he thoroughly despised and resented.

He found it hard to negotiate the give and take of life, finding there were more downs than ups. So, he constantly longed to escape to a dream world where he had, not only complete control, but also a sense of agency. At first, the mysterious ways in which people moved had interested him. But as he began to feel repeatedly battered rather than stimulated or comforted by others, his curiosity morphed into acute observation and analysis, eventually becoming contempt as he realised how predictable the self-indulgences were to which many individuals fell prey.

Years later, staring up at an unfamiliar ceiling from an unfamiliar bed, these worries slowly roused him from a very light sleep. Around him lay the remnants of the celebrations as the first rays of sunlight shone mercilessly through the thin cotton curtains.

It was still too early to contemplate getting up and facing the day, so Michael allowed his mind to wander as he stared at Helen. Finding an ashtray on her bedroom table, he lit up and continued to take in her beauty, unmarred by her sleep-clouded state. He was soon immersing himself in a haze of positives as happier memories took centre stage; positives which he tended to store away for these very rare occasions. For a while, his mood lifted as he allowed his lethargic mind to disconnect, sensing sleep had once more enveloped him.

Sometime in his late teens, Michael found himself, hammer and nails at hand, boarding up the spare bedrooms which, since his father's departure, had been a burden to maintain for him and his mother. With every strike of the hammer, Michael's grin grew wider. The fact his dad had insisted on keeping these rooms for guests was a source of further amusement for him since no one, neither friend or family, had ever stayed over — not even once.

Hammering nail after nail into the frames of the doors to leave each room emptied of furniture and fixtures to their respective fates, he began to chuckle. Soon his chuckles transformed into full-fledged laughter as he continued to take out his darker emotions on the doors with each swift blow of the hammer. He savoured the catharsis offered by strike after strike. Therefore, after completing his little task, he was left with a degree of disappointment whilst, at that same moment, he felt a weight lift from his shoulders.

Downstairs, he begrudgingly returned the hammer and leftover nails to their place inside a rusted, steel toolbox while he immersed himself in feelings of relief and freedom. At the kitchen table, his mother, smiling even wider than him, sipped at a mug of tea. Michael had a hot chocolate. Was his choice of brew sparked by a need to regress? He hadn't drunk hot chocolate in years, but, for once, Michael hardly cared. Mother and son were far too busy relishing their new-found freedom to allow the possibility of the suffocating gloom of their recent past to sabotage their elation.

Things were a lot less constrictive since the departure of their metaphorical "Big Brother". Would his father, if said, understand the choice of character Michael had adopted for him years previously? Right now, he also failed to care.

Although still asleep, Michael's over-active mind soon switched focus as he found himself grappling with one of his father's most prized fishing rods. This rebellious act was also one which he'd frequently savoured since his father's departure.

On the other end of the line, a large rainbow trout struggled with the hook buried deep inside its mouth. Michael used all the strength he could muster to keep the rod as steady as possible. He dealt out the occasional inch or so of line from the reel which jumped and jerked with every twitch of the trout's body.

Michael could relate to the ongoing fight for life. He understood not only the desperate pantomime acted out by hunter and hunted, but also the inevitable and necessary process of death: a death which would profit the hunter but cost the hunted its life. This creature lacked such self-awareness and had acted on an instinctual feeling of hunger. An instinct which had earnt it its death sentence. Caught in the drama of the moment, Michael was already looking forward to reeling in the now exhausted fish and watching its twitching body slowly lose its fight for life on the muddy riverbank.

Numerous times, his father had showed him how to kill quickly and humanely, and had even been told, rather hypocritically, that an instant death was preferable to the vile act of sadism he now exhibited. Watching the trout in its final throes of life, Michael smiled, but he also felt something growing around the area of his crotch. His face became flushed. All too quickly these physical responses cancelled each other as the trout twitched its last on the riverbank. Michael picked up the now limp body by the tail and returned it to the bubbling tributary. Job done.

He retraced his footsteps through the backyard, eventually sitting on the old rope swing beneath the ancient oak as it swung in the breeze while bearing the burden of his bulk.

Twenty-Six

Michael woke to remember the party, the house, the woman, and the position he was now in. Romantic liaisons didn't suit him, and he hoped Helen would view it as a one-night stand. He wasn't disappointed.

The look on her face when she turned over hardly required translation. Getting quickly dressed, he was out on the street again amongst the bottle rockets and streamers. He took a right down a narrow pathway branching off from the main drag and walked quarter of a mile until he reached a children's playground next to a football field. There, he settled onto one of the swings and studied the graffiti.

I didn't want to see Helen again, but still, there are ways of saying goodbye, he thought.

Breathing in the cold morning air, he lit up and inhaled until nicotine fired the nerve endings in his brain. He looked down at his hands and tobacco-stained fingers and recalled the oath he'd made to himself on St Andrews' pier.

Although the wound on his palm had healed, Michael still had a bandage around his hand to avoid awkward questions about the episode. Unwrapping it, he let the bandage fall to Earth and studied the scar. He dug his heels into the ground and stopped himself mid-swing. He felt like crying, screaming, laughing, but instead, he stayed silent. How could he let a New Year's Day rejection by a hungover stranger get right on top of him? He felt himself falling into a deep well, filled to the brim with suicidal thoughts and sadness, and at the bottom of which, peace and oblivion awaited. For a moment, he felt dizzy. Then he reminded himself this was just his second cigarette of the day. It was a filthy habit, but one he just couldn't seem to kick.

He left the playground, checking his watch as he pushed open the gate. It was coming up to nine in the morning and the streets would be empty for a while. Everyone would be sleeping off their hangovers. He picked his way through the post-party mess to his shabby B&B where he was confronted by a few hangers-on who were still drinking with his landlady in the kitchen.

"Late night?" she asked with a knowing smile.

"Early morning," he replied.

She invited him to join them, but he declined and took the rickety stairs up to his room to flop down on his bed. Thoughts returned of his suicide attempt back at the loch. Some people found life became more vivid when set against pain, suffering and trauma. That a nightmare made you appreciate a good night's sleep. That simple things such as sleep — dream and rumination-free — were what made life worth living. And that was what he wanted now. Forget the hours snatched this morning in someone else's bed. Forget the hours he could waste in something approaching a meditative trance, mulling things over, only to end up more exhausted than ever.

Part of the function of his rumination seemed to do with avoiding his problems. Often, he simply didn't recognise them. Just like someone with a troublesome character trait would deny its existence to a therapist, Michael would ignore his own thoughts until they manifested and morphed into emotions which were, in the main, unpleasant. Then he was left with feelings which he just didn't accept, leaving him dismissive, while awake and coherent of the emotions which were habitually ignored; emotions which also stood a very slim chance of being recognised.

As a youth, he had been accused of overthinking things, building problems up to be bigger than they were, and so, he had started preferring his own company.

It was a safer option than risking getting teased or bullied for being too introverted when he kept silent or being melodramatic when he voiced his fears. He had self-harmed, to some small degree, throughout his childhood. But that had mostly been attention-seeking rather than attempting to end his own life. These acts had been an attempt to convey to others how troubled he was. Instead, all he'd earnt was sympathy from his mother, derision from his peers and indifference and anger from his father and his teachers.

His mother had been the only one to act appropriately. Having caught him in the act or shortly afterwards, she would, while dressing his wounds, repeatedly ask him "Why?" Always, with a deadpan expression, he would answer, "Because it hurts."

Sometimes, first aid and sympathy had been enough to send these thoughts away, especially when his mother had given him her full attention, stroking his hair and talking soothingly to him. On other occasions, he'd want to lash out, scream, shout or curse. But he never did, not even when he was alone. Was it fear of his mother's image of God's omniscient eye? Or had he lost all respect for God's opinions? The devil seemed more real to him at those times.

He had been aware, even as a child, that the thoughts that occupied him were far heavier than normal. Most of his thinking had been done on that tired, old rope swing. Just conjuring up a vision of that oak tree brought back the thoughts themselves — good and bad — loud and clear.

Proper sleep eluded him but by early afternoon, Michael's mind had turned to more wholesome desires: fresh air on his face and an escape from his confined living space. Washed, dressed and, for once, motivated, he skirted the mess downstairs and picked through the still quiet streets to his car parked just off the high street. Unlocking it, he turned off the alarm, opened the door and sat behind the steering wheel.

The hills around the town would be the ideal location on this dreary New Year's afternoon, so he headed left and was soon surrounded by heather and peat. He'd harvested and eaten magic mushrooms in places such as this "back in the day" with fellow stoners. The trips had occasionally been good ones, but the majority had been bad.

Sometime in his early teens, Michael had trotted in at two in the morning, soaked in rain, with eyes dilated and his face bearing a classic junkie's pallor. His father had beaten him to within an inch of his life with the studded leather belt he kept handy for "special occasions". Michael thanked God he'd left the family home soon after.

He'd always been conflicted about his father, so much so that he hadn't even cried at the news of his death. On a purely biological level, Michael pondered whether he'd been born with faulty genes which meant the love between a father and a son had somehow failed to blossom between them. Had this happened congeniality at birth or, more likely, were fifteen years of constant abuse ultimately responsible?

He wondered how things would run if he had children. "The sins of the father are visited upon the son," the Bible proclaimed, but he considered the Bible to be full of shit. Preachers, ministers and priests followed its teachings blindly, even though half of its content and moral lessons had been debunked by modern science.

Politics made no sense to him either. Sometimes he felt he understood nothing about life, its structure and the individuals it comprised. He'd lost his mother, the only woman he'd ever loved. Where on earth could he rediscover that same degree of reciprocal affection? He had his head stuck in the past and felt no hope for salvation from other people since he regarded almost everybody with fear, cynicism and hate.

Depressed and jaded once more, he switched on the radio, got aggravated and switched it off again. He parked the car and began to walk in a landscape of rolling hills.

Michael pumped his legs hard uphill.

Now his mind was clear, he felt better able to focus on the scenery, and began to take in deep breaths of crisp mountain air. It was a tranquil place, but it would be easy to get lost so Michael kept a mental note of his position. He was used to losing chunks of time through drinking, so, at the very least, the walk would eat up part of the day and keep his mind free and serene as he walked.

It felt as though he was meeting more people here than out on the high street. Joggers, mountaineers and dog walkers made up the bulk, but there were some, like him, walking alone. Perhaps they too were free spirits caught up in their thoughts. He stopped to chat with a few and it lifted his mood. A problem shared *was* a problem halved, it would seem. His mother had always been fond of that saying and, while he walked, he ended up thinking about all the times his father had raised his hands to her.

At an early age, he'd assumed this to be the norm but as he grew older, in the late sixties, such behaviour began to be frowned upon. *I was born ten years too early*, he thought as he walked. Given time, he could have been spared, by laws and new social norms, the beatings he had been subjected to, and which his mother had been powerless to stop. The only consolation he'd received was the love which she had displayed towards him afterwards. Sadly, hugs and kisses could do little to heal bruises.

Michael spat on the ground. Irritated once again, he headed back to his car, switched on the radio and sat in the driver's seat for a while. An old T-Rex number followed by the on-the-hour news: war, gang violence, murder as well as "niceties" aimed at lightening the state of the world's problems, snippets of celebrity gossip, royal engagements and whatever else was circulating on the "grapevine" of the lives of the rich, famous and frivolous. It all stole another hour out of his day.

He switched off the radio and drove back to town, trying to keep his mood steady as he left the mountains behind. After returning to his room and with nothing to do but sleep, he realised he had managed a whole day without booze. He crashed out on his bed and any feelings of withdrawal were soon replaced, once more, by thoughts relating to his mother.

Twenty-Seven

L ater into his teens — and despite the fact Michael was using drugs and drinking too much — his mother continued to provide a safe haven for her son. For her, "Mummy's little soldier" also provided a source of comfort whenever things went awry with her abusive yet seemingly loyal husband. Until he had departed altogether — and even after that — his father never once strayed, as far as Michael could tell. Although his raging tempers might suggest inflamed passions, these seemed to be confined to his negative states rather than being deflected into sexual thoughts or acts outside the marriage. In this way, his abuse was solely inflicted on his intimate family. Michael was different from him in this respect, as his sexual activities were frequent and usually acquired with cold hard cash.

Michael was sure this unchanneled sexual energy, which Freud had labelled the libido, added extra impetus to his frequent bouts of discipline. But even if this was the case, what use was understanding in the end? Despite all the thinking and analysing he undertook, especially in relation to his father, it could do nothing to alter the way he had behaved. In relation to himself, maybe at times his over-active libido gave him some sort of release from the violent predispositions which his father had modelled for him. But who knew, really? At least Michael seemed to have either inherited or chosen to model himself on his mother, with her easy-going nature and forgiving philosophy.

Michael felt the urge to weep. He hadn't totally accepted the loss of his mother but when it came down to it, her death had released him from the guilt of harbouring unforgiving and un-Christian thoughts towards his father, which had always been forbidden by her.

As sleep took hold, there were no fires, no beatings, no punishments or chores, just the rolling, meandering countryside of his hometown. His dream was filled with nothing but peace and harmony as he watched on as a mere observer, sensing a fresh breeze caress his face, neck and torso. So it remained for what seemed like hours until, despite the tranquillity of the dreamscape, he sensed a sudden shift in mood. Subconsciously, Michael mouthed the words, "Spare the rod and spoil the child."

Still caught up in a dream, he was reminded that the saying was one of his father's favourites; one which he had uttered during lashings from his studded belt. He'd even encouraged corporal punishment with a cane from Michael's old schoolmaster who'd delivered each stroke with the same malicious smile his father had sported every time he strayed from the "straight and narrow". For an indeterminable time, Michael dreamt a dream of unfettered hostility but, eventually — and not a moment too soon — he awoke. Fully dressed, he sauntered to the window and sat on a rickety stool while watching passing traffic. He was so calm it verged on lethargy.

He watched for a while, noting the peace and serenity of the afternoon lull. And then he began to daydream. Soon finding himself immersed in a familiar memory whose initial manifestation always presented itself with the sound of a dripping tap. He was only half-conscious, but its source was obvious. It was the old cold water tap in the bathroom which was badly in need of a washer.

Opening his eyes, young Michael pulled on his pyjama bottoms and, naked from the waist up, crossed the hallway. The bathroom door was, as usual, slightly ajar due to the heat of the months expanding the wooden frame and ensuring some force was required to close it properly.

He pushed it open and witnessed something that would haunt him for the rest of his life. His father was sitting in the tub, facing the wall and whistling softly to himself. On his back, a multitude of scars crisscrossed from left to right and up and down.

Standing in the doorway, breathing as softly as he could, Michael began to understand the darker aspects of human nature for the first time in his life. He was fourteen years of age. Pretty soon, he felt rage rising as butterflies flew around his stomach. As his blood began to boil, he slowly realised the source of his father's rage and general impatience.

It took a victim to become a victimiser.

What he wanted then, despite his anger, was to embrace his father and to tell him that all could be forgiven. But his empathy was soon overridden by the rage he felt in the deep pit of his stomach, and soon he was backtracking across the landing and down the stairs via the rickety staircase.

Twenty-Eight

Following his short-lived but intense daydream, Michael felt a desire to leave. Just as in Blackpool, his current home had triggered unasked for memories which had left him tired and irritable. St Andrews itself was placid but he'd been annoyed in equal measure by his daydream, his landlady's party, the noisiness of inner city hedonists and the nosiness of the suburbanites. He had paid for his current accommodation weekly and was free to leave, preferring to lose a little money rather than having to face any awkward questions.

Packing up his things, he left the room key on the kitchen counter and got behind the wheel of his car. He was almost out of petrol, cigarettes and alcohol, and so stepped on the accelerator. Catching a glimpse of himself in the mirror, he saw that he looked as rough as he felt after last night's booze-up.

Stopping at the local self-service station, he pumped in forty pounds worth of fuel and then used the ATM.

Drawing out a hundred pounds, he paid at the counter and got himself two large bottles of Scotch and a few packets of Marlboro cigarettes.

Back in his car, he unscrewed the top of one of the bottles, took a large mouthful and swallowed. Placing it back inside its carrier bag, he exited the station and, once clear of its grounds, lit a cigarette as he switched on the radio. Nothing but news, news and more news battered him so he selected a random tape from the glovebox: a Bob Dylan album, and, while he listened to the lyrics of "Maggie's Farm", found it too politically charged for his current state of mind. He knew it would land him a serious headache so he continued on in silence until he pulled into a parking lot of a town surrounded by another larger loch. Without realising, he had driven to a similar spot to the one where he had attempted to drown himself. This time though, he decided to find a warm, comfortable B&B where he could get his head down for a few hours and then sample the hospitality of the local pubs.

After locking the car, Michael walked along the main thoroughfare where a multitude of "vacancy" signs greeted him. He selected one at random, strode through the entrance and rang the bell at the reception desk. The sound of a TV showing the evening soaps could be heard whilst a tall and gangly teenager materialised behind the desk.

"Looking for a room?" he asked in his breaking voice.

Michael nodded.

"Hang on!" the youth exclaimed, hurrying inside what Michael assumed was the television room for paying guests.

Business must have been slow because, as Michael peered through the doorway, he could see that the woman he assumed to be the landlady was also watching TV in there. She was rather overweight and sporting a ponytail some twenty years too young for her. At the desk, they arranged for Michael to stay for a week.

"A week?" she said with surprise.

Michael responded in the affirmative.

"Not a problem."

He only had his satchel, to which he had added two bottles of the finest Scotch and a few packets of cigarettes.

"Is there a smoking room?" he asked without much hope.

The woman, Christine — or Chris for short — replied, "I'll get you an ashtray as long as you smoke near the window. You won't offend any of the guests in the communal room. There aren't any."

Michael noticed the pound signs in Chris' eyes as he paid in full but didn't respond to her obvious greed. The room was small but comfortable and he slumped down on the bed and closed his eyes.

Twenty-Nine

On the verge of sleep, Michael's mind proceeded to take him back to his previous thoughts on what, in later life, he would label the "bathroom incident". He stood tall, high on adrenaline and anger as he backtracked down the staircase, hall and on into the kitchen. Crossing its chequered floor, he walked towards the knife block and selected one at random.

Returning to the bathroom, he screamed at the top of his lungs and cut deep into the palm of his left hand. What happened next dumbfounded him. His father wrapped a nearby towel around his waist and, stepping into the blood which now soaked the floor at his feet, wrapped both of his arms around him, dressing the wound with a flannel.

He apologised time and time again.

From that point on, the beatings ceased. However, Michael knew deep inside his father's head, hostility continued to reign. Whether his father truly loved him or not, Michael knew that fundamentally his dad's outlook on life wouldn't change. Whenever he happened to come across him in the house, his eyes seemed indifferent, almost dead. Once more, he came to the conclusion that his dad was so twisted and insecure that his level of wickedness could be measured by Michael on an almost biblical scale. Years of experience had also taught him that his brand of evil wasn't rare; it resided within the minds of other men similar to his father. Nothing but love, he'd once assumed, could eliminate such distortions. But, at fourteen, he became disabused of the notion, coming to the unwavering conclusion that some people simply couldn't or wouldn't be helped and that giving up on them and snubbing them out of your own life was the sanest, kindest course of action to take.

He thought about this while reflecting on the "bathroom incident". An episode that was regularly grasped by his conscious mind from the store of incidents which constituted his long-term memory. Still, he now had his present and future to occupy himself with. *No more soul-destroying thoughts*, he promised himself whilst he groaned himself awake on the bed in his rented room.

Thirty

It was unusual to be staying in a B&B without a television in each room. Worried that without the distraction he would start over-thinking, Michael slipped on his jacket at around seven in the evening, felt for his wallet and left to step out into the rain.

The heavens had opened and, by the time he'd reached the nearest pub, he was wet to his core. Standing in The Black Friar, he removed his jacket and shook off the rain. The place was empty; not even anyone behind the bar. He rang the last orders bell to get some attention. A woman in her early twenties eventually appeared. She rated a moderate five out of ten on his attractiveness scale, but after a few drinks, she had moved up to a healthy seven or eight.

Considering the age gap between them, he felt like a dirty old man and yet he continued to ruminate on her attractiveness, and even started debating whether he should buy her a drink or two. She barely conversed with him and avoided all eye contact. Being a barmaid, she must have had all sorts of creeps hitting on her on a nightly basis. Anyway, due to his current condition, he realised in any conversation they could have had, he would undoubtedly find himself slurring his way through all of his vowels.

Nine o'clock. With a full two hours to make a fool out of himself, he switched his poison from whisky to beer and, as usual, drank and drank until the bar felt rickety and the stool he sat on felt incapable of holding his weight.

Mumbling a "goodbye" to Sharon — or was it Sheila? — Michael made his way homeward, head spinning and toppling over onto the pavement after only a few strides. Swaying, he just about managed to let himself through the front door of the B&B before falling again, this time head-first onto the reception's rough carpeting. Luckily, no one was around, but as he made his way up the stairs, he had to keep a firm grip on the banister. Letting himself in to his room, he collapsed onto his bed while the room span around him. Sleep came quickly; its fast transition helped along by a glut of alcohol ensuring he passed out rather than drifted off.

Thirty-One

Following the "bathroom Incident", he admitted nothing of the violence he had performed upon himself to the nurse who had stitched up his hand. Instead, he said something about a fishing accident, the line slipping as he reeled in his latest catch and cutting into his palm as he let go of the rod.

"Must've been a big fish," she said.

"Seemed like it," he replied, smiling pleasantly at her whilst she handed him a lollipop, which he'd thought, at the age of fourteen, was a little patronising. Aside from that, he was glad to have endured the condescension as it confirmed the fact she'd swallowed his story. Along with a few antibiotics, a doctor prescribed him a strip of very strong painkillers which had sent his head spinning and put a smile on his face.

That had been his first real taste of drugs and their effects. Maybe it had also been the real start of his problems. Maybe all that Freudian crap about parent-child relationships hadn't applied to him. Perhaps Michael's first taste of morphine had been his downfall because barely half a dozen years later, during one of his darker moments, he'd actively re-sought its euphoric effects.

Years later, he'd expressed this view to a group of junkies whose sole purpose in life had been the acquisition of their next fix. Their reaction had either been silence or feigned sympathy. Michael had preferred the silence; the pretension only really irritated him. But pretence or not, talking with this group about even the most mundane of subjects did become therapeutic. After several months of mutual soul-searching, he had left the group believing he'd found a cure for his addictions.

He'd been wrong. Despite a decades-old promise to himself, Michael had not just tripped and fallen off the proverbial wagon but had got himself mangled-up underneath its wheels to boot. Perhaps he also harboured a masochistic streak. Something which his dead grandfather had passed down to him; scars inflicted from grandfather to son to grandson.

Although his father had seemed to specialise more in sadism than masochism, who knew what self-harming thoughts might have gone on inside his head?

Why dwell on this though? he thought, but for him the answer was elusive. Certainly, pain and suffering seemed always to come hand-in-hand with love and joy.

Thirty-Two

When he awoke from a short sleep, Michael got up and started smoking at the half-open window. Things were quiet in these very early hours so, in the absence of any other form of distraction, he found himself focusing on his father's sweet departure from the family home.

Although Michael's father had habitually shifted blame from himself to his wife and son, his eventual departure, Michael realised, must have been precipitated by some sort of conscience, however elusive. He must have harboured feelings of guilt, however deeply buried, to the point his actual home, full as it was of constant reminders of his abuse, became unbearable. Another possibility was he had also started to view his own behaviour as deviant, and he realised he simply wasn't fit to be in any sort of relationship.

And yet Michael realised that, after he had left, he had missed his father. Despite the beatings, he had shared intimate moments with him, such as the intense bonding sessions where he had educated him on aspects of life and had granted him the gift of intellect through literature. Whilst thinking about these times, Michael guessed he was on the way to forgiving his dad, something which he could hardly believe and which he certainly wouldn't have admitted to anybody else.

However, with his father making his living in London and safely out of his and his mother's lives, the baton had been passed to Michael's headmaster.

Whilst the absence of his father was a bonus, the caring nature of his mother was still something he wallowed in whenever he was beaten by the brutish headmaster. One such occasion followed the theft of the spare key to the school's main door, which had hung safely on a chain inside the main office.

At that time, halfway through a beating, the principal had been distracted by a fire drill which was held about once a month and required all staff and pupils to gather at the entrance to the school. He was distracted for only a few seconds, but it was time enough for Michael to snatch the key and its chain and deposit it inside his neatly pressed school trousers. What would he actually do with it? At present, he didn't quite know, but, at some future time, he was sure it would become useful.

Another two or three copies, he knew, were entrusted to the school cleaner and a few members of staff who were in the habit of being early starters. Therefore, the missing key might only be noticed days, maybe even weeks, later as the headmaster hardly ever arrived before one of the other key-holders had already opened up.

Soon though, Michael and his persecutor were standing at the school gates while a supply teacher started to count heads as the siren-like fire bell was silenced. Then, when everything was kosher, most of the school's pupils filed their way back past him to their respective classes. Michael though, was grabbed by the collar and escorted back to endure the rest of his beating.

Back in the present, Michael felt disinclined to continue these thoughts. It was still the very early morning hours and, while he smoked, he wished for the more pleasant dreams that involved the better sides of his life, like the intimate aspects of his relationships with the opposite sex which mostly arose, he'd admit, on the back of cold hard cash. So, at four in the morning, all of these recollections gradually relinquished their hold on him and, still sitting on the same chair by the window, he looked out at the streetlights of the town and the moonlit loch beyond them.

He continued to light cigarette after cigarette by the half-open window as he sat, hypnotised by the view, for a few hours more.

Eventually, there came the sound of activity outside his room. The smell of brewing coffee and whispered conversation emanating from the kitchen preceded by a rapping on his door and the call to breakfast. Michael was hungry so he made his way down to the breakfast table where he proceeded to stuff himself with toast and cereal. Afterwards, he took a shower, dressed and lay fully clothed on his bed. He slept until ten, then took hold of his jacket and made his way outside.

The weather was cold and wet as Michael made his way through the town, kicking the rain-soaked cobbles until he eventually sat on a bench facing the loch. He found himself staring out at the choppy waters, transfixed by the view. After an hour or so, he walked back through the same streets and into the nearest bar. At first, he stuck to cola and played his favoured list of contemporary and seventies tunes on the jukebox. There he stayed until about two in the afternoon before returning to the B&B to sit in the television room where he found himself watching an old black and white movie. For once, he began to crave human contact but for at least an hour or so, he was denied. Then Chris strolled in, sat by him and sipped at a brew with an entire packet of Rich Tea biscuits. She sat there for a while, stuffing her face and offering him a cup of tea every few minutes. However, Michael was caffeinated enough thanks to the gallon of cola he'd drunk at the bar.

Having lost all interest in the film and his temporary landlady, he yawned his way back to his room. Still needing to catch up after his early morning awakening, he proceeded to recollect decades-old memories involving that rusty, old key.

Thirty-Three

On a cool, cloudless day shortly after his fourteenth birthday and slightly before his father's departure, Michael rocked himself back and forth on the rope swing. His stitched hand was a little sore but the pain was focusing his attention away from his lethargic state of mind.

He'd hardly slept because he'd made use of the stolen key in the early hours. At around three, he had walked through the deserted streets to the schoolhouse, approaching along the lane to the rear of the building then skirting around it to the main front door which was flanked by an imposing gateway. Adrenaline had coursed through his body as he had placed the key in the lock. Surreptitiously, Michael had twisted it and pushed the door with his shoulder, nudging it open as it creaked on its hinges to allow him to enter the sick funhouse designated as a place of *education* but which felt more like a place of *subjugation*.

A world of possibilities stood before him.

His first thought was to head along the corridor to the headmaster's office, but he found himself side-tracked by the urge to just stroll the empty classrooms and corridors of the main building, pausing now and then as memories flooded him. It was pitch black, but Michael didn't dare switch on any lights in case a passer-by, or even the police, might be alerted.

Outside of school, he hadn't crossed paths with the law, but, he supposed, when peer pressure wasn't an issue, you tended not to break laws. If anything, he was more likely to be a victim rather than a perpetrator, his present trespasses aside.

Exhilarated and slightly exhausted, he eventually arrived at the principal's office. His mood lifted as he crossed the threshold, for once not facing punishment but instead seeking reparation.

Leaning in a corner was that dreaded wooden cane. Michael cried out in anger and grasped hold of its shaft and snapped it in two across his knee. He threw the remnants across the desk and, now crying uncontrollably, left the office and then the schoolhouse, making sure to lock the door behind him.

Back on the old rope swing, these memories dissipated as he focused on his present situation. He had just witnessed his mother take yet another beating. Tears and pain. The stitches in his hand had begun to loosen, letting blood seep out. It spattered on the rope while, high above him, storm clouds began to form.

He'd have to return to the house soon or else suffer a beating of the like his mother had just endured. He crossed the garden and stepped through the rear door as the first spatters of rain pummelled the windows. He ran to his room and pulled his bed against the door before falling onto it and wiping the last of the tears from his eyes. A knock at the door set his heart pounding. The door handle turned.

"Mikey?" His mother's voice. "It's all right, Mikey. He's gone." Her voice was strained; she almost seemed to stutter.

Michael felt rage bubbling up inside him, but concern for his mother calmed him. Pulling his bed clear, he opened the door and let his bruised and battered mum into the room. There they stayed, embracing and shedding tears together after his father had slammed the front door on his way out to the pub or off-licence.

Michael suspected his father would die young as a result of his drinking. But as it turned out, it would be his mother who suffered a premature death. Fifteen years on, her only release, cigarettes, would kill her with a tumour which, by that time of her life, was the size of a tennis ball but soon branched off from her chest to spread through the rest of her body. Her death came as her adult life had been: painful and tortuous. Michael had ended up hating his father even more than he hated God and that was saying something.

In this dream state, Michael was held back from the present and future, tied to dual fantasies of vengeful feelings towards his father and forgiveness and love for his mother. He was trapped ruminating on the rope swing as he was in his adult life but being well aware of the fact took nothing away from its frequent manifestation and he awoke pondering it all. Feeling lost, he came to the realisation his dreams were becoming more and more vivid whilst memories competed to secure a spot at the forefront of his mind.

The clock on the wall now read a quarter past seven. All that drink, even the thought of it, was making him feel nauseous. He opened the window fully, knelt in front of it and furnished his lungs with another hefty dose of fresh air. The urge to vomit abated and so, deciding to fill rather than empty his stomach, he took a short walk to what had now become his local for a pub dinner.

At The Black Friar, he ordered and sat at a table. His food arrived and he ate with gusto, ignoring the curious looks of the rest of the pub's punters. It was obviously a locals' pub during the off-season so who was this stranger in their midst? A pint washed down the eight-ounce steak and he returned to the bar for another drink.

A man introduced himself as Jeff.

"What's your name?" he asked.

"Mike."

An inconsequential, bland session of questions and answers followed, resulting in goodbyes, more beer, and a descent into oblivion.

Later, back in his room, everything around him began to spin. Michael closed his eyes but it did nothing to help and so he got up, once again, to kneel in front of the window and breathe in a few lungfuls of fresh air to clear his head. Craving complete sobriety, Michael hit the "on" switch at the base of the room's kettle. He watched on hypnotised while it boiled. All too suddenly the red light illuminating the switch went dead, signalling the availability of boiling water. Michael moved to the small table, got himself a cup and proceeded to tip almost every sachet of the free coffee available into it. After adding the water, he stirred and drank it black.

Soon the coffee and fresh air coming through the window had sobered him enough to counter the spinning in his head. He continued to stare out of the window towards the high street and, in the distance, towards the loch. Once more, he found himself enveloped in predictable, regressive memories.

Thirty-Four

His mother had not gone out much while his father was around as her husband regarded himself as patriarch and bread-winner, and wished to keep that role. If she had done, Michael was certain things would have turned out better. She could have sought the networks and support she needed to give her strength to leave or, at least, challenge his behaviour. Friends were a no-no and she was tied to the sink and cooker for as long as his dad deemed it necessary.

She had been sheepish, nervous and insecure which, Michael understood much later, were classic signs of abuse. He'd gone through the same tendencies but had always vowed to fight the tortures his father put him through, mentally at least. When he had cried, he had started to regard it as a sign of strength rather than weakness, since he knew how much it had angered his father. It had become a source of consolation, not shame.

He had understood in his early teens that his father was a bully and a tyrant, and also where his behaviour had originated. His paternal grandfather must have taught him how to deal out abuse on a routine basis and his father must also have suffered the same physical and mental abuse he meted out to Michael.

Out on the back porch, his mother smoked almost incessantly but Michael didn't mind as he had also developed the habit and smoked alongside her. His father had gone and for the first time in years, she smiled and tousled his hair while staring into the distance, thinking her own thoughts. The atmosphere was calm, and nothing could intrude on their bond. Right now, nothing needed to be said, as they stared at the setting sun. Their companionable silence expressed freedom and relief. Having had the mortgage fully paid years earlier, his mother had taken possession of the house and was working at a bakery to cover bills and maintain the property's upkeep.

Stubbing out his cigarette, Michael got up and embraced his mum. She whispered softly into his ear, "I love you… and I'm sorry."

"He should be sorry," Michael replied, adding, "But I think he's only half-sorry and mostly for himself."

"Should've done more," she said with conviction.

But Michael was sure there was nothing she could have done. The love they shared, and could express without hindrance, was unaltered. The tears Michael shed, as he rested his head on his mother's shoulder, were tears of mutual joy rather than those of mutual pain and despair.

Part Three

Thirty-Five

Whether she fell or was pushed was a moot point because that fall signalled the eventual end of things. His father was formally charged but the charges were dropped when his mother refused to cooperate with the police. Michael knew the truth though. She had been pushed.

His mother was in plaster for months, with casts around her right arm and leg. Bones tended to heal slower with age, and those first few months were a constant reminder of his father's actions. Each time Michael saw him surreptitiously glance in her direction, he was sure his dad's conscience had finally kicked in. But he seemed to resent his own actions, suggesting he was suffering from self-pity rather than guilt. He was playing the blame game and was soon packing his bags and leaving his mother and him with the house and whatever savings he'd transferred into her bank account over the years. His destination? London, where he eventually applied for work on the Stock Exchange.

Despite the substantial savings she'd acquired, his mother enjoyed her new job. She soon developed several friendships but didn't ever discuss her treatment at the hands of her husband. She was old-fashioned like that, preferring instead to excuse his actions. On some level, she seemed to even consider herself partly to blame. Having taken on-board taunts, jibes and slurs, maybe she'd ended up believing what his dad had always told her. The doubts he had cast about her always diligent housekeeping, her intelligence and even her own fidelity, the latter through using words like slut or whore. Michael believed otherwise, because he had an outsider's perspective on his mother's insecurity and the depth of his dad's malice.

Since Michael had been his father's little, part-time, study project and shared fifty percent of his genes, he recognised the risk of him becoming ten times the tyrant his dad had been. But whether it was through nurture, nature or a combination was unimportant. What *was* important was the fact he had always striven to fight against the corrupt elements of his psyche.

Back in bed at his temporary Scottish home, Michael admonished himself.

"Snap out of it, Mikey," he said to himself, and was soon reaching for a cigarette. He inhaled deeply, providing his battered lungs with another hefty dose of nicotine and tar. What he would do with the rest of the day he didn't know, but he decided to avoid the pub. It was too early to drink, even for him. Today, he preferred keeping a clear head, so, slipping on his trainers, he decided on a walk along the loch.

A slight breeze had begun to blow in from the west, and the clouds above him were threatening rain. He could hear thunder crackling in the distance as a storm front seemed about to engulf the small hamlet. The bad weather now precluded his walk along the loch and so he backtracked through the cobbled streets to a cafe where he ordered a full English and sat staring out of the window with a strong cup of coffee while he waited for his food to arrive.

The place was deserted, and Michael wondered why they stayed open at all. Whereas in Blackpool, they tended to shut the cafes in the off-season, here, they were clearly struggling for trade yet remained stubbornly in business. At least this little place seemed unaffected by Blackpool's underbelly of crime, addiction, homelessness, prostitution and gambling. But, for some, that was what attracted them to the town where sex, drugs and vice in all of its forms served as a given to an ever-growing select few — people not unlike Michael.

The bell above the entrance to the cafe rattled into life.

Michael glanced over his shoulder as the new arrival went past. She was attractive, with a nice figure discernible under a baggy woollen cardigan and equally baggy jeans. After sitting at a table facing him, she nursed a coffee and stared out the window, much as he had done. Eventually, she glanced in his general direction. Michael offered a smile as a substitute for "hello" but she greeted it with almost catatonic indifference.

When Michael's food arrived, he made quick work of it. Feeling awkward and a little embarrassed, he paid his bill and left.

The town's main thoroughfare was completely deserted. Only his thoughts filled the vacuum as he sat on the low bench facing the loch. The choppy waters whipped into waves and crashed against the shoreline. Once again, his mind was drowned in memory as he slipped into recollections of the painful demise of his mother.

She had died at a young age.

Her daily dose of twenty cigarettes had caught up with her in her mid-fifties. His father hadn't attended her funeral. Out of guilt, Michael surmised. But Michael had been there, crying his heart out and cursing his own nicotine habit. He had always valued his mother's life above his own. Like his father, she had no siblings and with his grandparents long gone, Michael had been the only one of her bloodline in attendance. Her life insurance had left him financially comfortable, but her emotional influence was still sorely missed.

His school days had ended a few short months after his father's departure, but what sweetened the deal and provided Michael with a small compensation for his treatment, was the fact the school and his headmaster's career had gone the way of all things. The final nail in its coffin was the jailing of the principal for using excessive and violent force on not only Michael, but also on numerous other pupils.

The place had soon become an eyesore, with graffiti sprayed on its walls, and acts of criminal damage plainly visible: broken and boarded-up windows, rotting timber frames and missing roof slates. Just recently, since leaving St Andrews anyway, Michael had found himself feeling an almost overwhelming elation whenever he recalled his own contribution to the building's final demise. Running over such memories, despite the trespass and the arson, now seemed to lift his mood. The feelings of release even came close to the sensations he experienced during a drug-clouded high, or with the memories of his mother.

His thoughts were interrupted by the realisation he was no longer alone. Her approach must have been lost behind the combination of his introspection and the sound of the waves crashing along the shore.

"Business or pleasure?"

Michael turned his head and found himself looking into the eyes of the woman he'd smiled at in the cafe.

"Sorry?" he asked.

She shook her head and offered him her hand. "Where's my manners? I'm Kate. So, are you here on business or pleasure?"

Feeling a sense of déjà-vu, Michael shook her hand and said, "Not sure yet. I'm Michael, by the way."

She smiled. "Michael... Mike?"

"If you like," he returned.

That was how it got started. Although well used to talking to strangers, Michael was wary — not least because of the badge she sported on her jacket. It was an outline of a fish, an old Christian symbol originally denoting faith, since the disciples had been fishermen.

Kate and Michael ended up sitting together on the edge of the bench, staring out towards the loch and talking about nothing in particular. Despite his reservations,

Michael found himself glad of the company. They saw dog walkers, joggers and out-of-towners passing by, and acknowledged them all with a friendly wave.

Why she was talking to him at all was probably due to the fact she was a practising Christian and was interested in either swaying his beliefs or helping him in some way. Michael remained careful. Having opened up his feelings to drug addicts, a prostitute and countless other inebriates, he shouldn't have been even slightly fazed, but in his sober disposition, the cat seemed to have got his tongue.

He soon gleaned a detailed account of Kate's life so far, which included her first few years at Edinburgh University studying theology. Following this, she had returned home to this sleepy township to take care of her ailing mother, who had passed away just under a year ago.

Gradually, a shift to gentler subjects compelled Michael himself to talk, and he slowly found himself elaborating on an upbringing filled with the consoling, constant love of his mother. Contrary to his earlier thoughts, he also found himself recollecting in vivid detail the lowest parts of his life, but he said nothing of the abuse dealt to him by his father.

But Kate hardly seemed to notice the potential of his mood changing as she continued to chat about being stuck in the same wide-space-in-the-road where she had spent most of her twenty-five years of life.

"It's a nice place to visit," she said, "But it's a bore to live in."

Michael, knowing a lot about boredom, nodded and said, "Sometimes it's not the place but the people living in it."

Kate agreed and sat in silence for a moment before adding, "Your life belongs to others here."

Michael urged her to go.

"You can't even sneeze here without half the town knowing within an hour."

Michael smiled.

"Most of the town have been asking about you already," she added.

He sighed. "You're a scout then?"

"No. I happen to be the welcoming party."

Michael laughed and she joined in. A simple truth eased his over-active mind, and he mulled it over as the conversation continued. Kate shifted her focus, bringing on a deluge of questions which Michael, slightly less fazed, began to answer in an almost robotic fashion.

As they talked, positive thoughts pushed back against the more troubling recollections that had scarred his outlook and opinion of the world. Just an hour or two of conversation seemed to have positively affected his jaded perspective. Would it be premature to see this short interaction as a panacea to his self-destructive journey? Perhaps he had been welcoming death through alcohol, tobacco and drugs. But maybe, by talking to someone who seemed to care, he discovered he might actually be seeking salvation. He'd been uncaring to himself and too many others, not only during the past few months, but throughout his life. Seeing himself as a "good guy" was hard for even him to consider, let alone accept, and consequently his already battered self-esteem had been further damaged.

Things were fine until Kate started talking about God in "all of his guises". Michael changed the subject by telling her he wasn't exactly a "God-fearing" person, but she countered by asking what he did believe in. He replied with silence, and that was that for a while.

It had been a good few months since he'd left his hometown and bumped into Lisa at the start of his journey and then Claire in Glasgow. In a small Scottish town, there wasn't much of a red-light district and the drug scene was practically non-existent, so why he'd come here at all was a mystery even to him. Maybe fate had a part to play. Kate had approached and engaged with him somewhat out-of-the-blue, which, even in a generally friendly Scottish town, seemed unusual. But he supposed it was just another link in the chain his life had become and it was then that he snatched the memory of his father crying on the beach in Blackpool. He felt he trusted Kate and, for once, was comfortable enough to talk about it.

"Was it down to a random burst of emotion, do you think? Or might it have been connected to some memory he was having, related to that place?" he asked tentatively.

She had no answer though and shook her head.

Still, the question remained hanging and Michael found himself slipping into a nagging state of denial that made him feel weak and impotent. What had caused this feeling? For once, he had no idea. He was stumped, and so ceased thinking about it. The conversation had also hit a brick wall and so, with a small hint of hope for future relations, they parted company. He tracked his way back to the B&B where he fell back onto his bed and stared up at the Artex ceiling.

Thirty-Six

It was a grey mid-week January day during his mid-twenties and Michael found himself pondering on a simple fact: hanging around with unscrupulous bastards was par-for-the-course when you made the conscious decision to become a junkie. Other arguments might counter such a course of action wasn't conscious at all. These ran along the lines that free will often took second place next to factors such as habit, dependency and addiction. Michael was no angel, but ripping off friends and family because of your own self-inflicted habits was low, and nobody but the selfish and self-absorbed, attempting to excuse their actions, would think otherwise.

He had enjoyed the effects of a multitude of drugs in his younger years and, as far as he was concerned, that was the only factor that had caused his addictions; a word he still hesitantly used. Some would cite neglect and abuse, especially during childhood, as the main cause of their drug-clouded existence and inability to form and maintain normal and natural run-of-the-mill lives. But, sitting as he was now, in a circle with his junkie "friends", airing and sharing such memories, Michael grasped how pathetic they all sounded. Until it was his turn. He found himself doing exactly the same, recalling in vivid detail his and his mother's treatment at the hands of his father. Even as he opened up, he clung to the thrill of self-conscious, detached, low-key self-absorption he detected on the face of every single soul gathered there. His disclosure continued. He felt there had been no choice but to go there, to play along. And yet he had ended up bearing his soul to those whose addictions had earnt them court-appointed "interventions" and prescriptions for habit-breaking drugs, such as methadone.

Michael told himself he was there simply because being around others of his kind was preferable to one-on-one counselling sessions, which would give him nowhere to hide. At least here, he could consider himself superior to those who seemed to share his own afflictions. The only downside was it ended up taking up a large part of his day. On the other hand, the upside had been that, up to that point at least, he had only listened and not been obliged to share.

He digested the plights of these people, all of whom had been either beaten, neglected or abused throughout their childhoods. It was mostly men. Women tended to open up more generally, chatting about nothing in particular, gossiping about acquaintances and friends, sharing snippets about their own lives. Men, he found, were keen to keep their feelings locked away by surrounding themselves within a bullshit persona of masculinity.

Michael continued to share until, much to his surprise, he found he was crying. He told himself he had been caught up in self-pity; caught up in his own story. He'd found himself bearing his soul to those around him. What was also surprising was the fact he now couldn't help but feel some sort of loose connection with those whose background, habits and pitfalls he shared.

Somehow, talking became a release, but as he began to digest the fact, waves of guilt clouded his mind. His inaction was the primary cause: guilt at his failure to prevent his father's abuse. But his mother's unflinching forgiveness of his father became a growing source of anger. Why it mattered now, he failed to understand. But he continued to weep and talk, shedding tears as those around him either nodded or shook their heads in feigned sympathy.

His earlier thoughts had touched upon what could be called "liberalism". But these faded now, along with his feelings of superiority. Michael realised the physical pain inflicted upon him by his father and members of his school's faculty had taken second place behind the emotional pain which, unknowingly, he had carried on his back for so long. He felt a loose affinity with these strangers and for the first time in years, his self-absorption took a back seat to sympathy for others.

This sympathy, unexpected as it was, conspired to dull his views on the human condition as he had understood it. One thing that prevailed was the image of his scarred father lying in the bathtub whistling softly to himself, blissfully unaware of his son's emotional state as he looked on. A dawning realisation hit him square between the eyes. It seemed that, as he had often thought since, victims became victimisers and those who were hurt often came to hurt others. It was a very philosophical way to end that day's session but as those around him made their way out of the room, which during the week doubled as a lecture theatre, Michael felt more like a victim than a survivor.

Drying his eyes, he felt the hand of the therapist on his shoulder. A shiver tore through him, but he managed to hold the tears back this time. As he said his goodbyes, he looked back and sensed not just a dawning realisation of his emotional state but also a realisation that a problem shared was often a problem halved.

Back in the present, he decided he was through with chasing ghosts. *All I have is the here and now*, he thought as he unwrapped the bandage on his hand. The knife had cut deep but the wound itself was on the verge of completely healing. He remembered the oath he'd made to himself: that he would kill himself by the end of the year. If his self-destructive habits had not already done the job. Suddenly, he began to feel depressed. Surely there was more to life than waiting for your turn to die. With the thoughts of his earlier therapy sessions in mind, he decided to find himself a different kind of tonic which wouldn't require drinking or drugging himself into oblivion.

Where she'd be, he didn't know, but based on their conversation that morning, he was as sure as hell he wouldn't find Kate anywhere near a bar. It was the second time that day he'd found an excuse not to drink, and in truth, he felt the better for it. Talking to someone who gave a damn would also make a pleasant change; his chance meeting with Kate had given him a taste for it. So, after dousing his hand with medicinal alcohol and putting on a clean bandage, he went scouting for her next to the small age-battered bench. It was an hour or so before he caught sight of her walking a sheepdog near the shoreline. She glanced in his direction and, slightly warily he sensed, she approached.

For a while, Michael's only motivation that day had been the pursuit of a hefty dose of alcohol and his daily ration of thirty cigarettes. But now he sensed another chance at redemption. His need to speak with Kate was connected to him recognising her as an outlet for his thoughts and feelings. Although it seemed very premature, Michael had sensed a class of goodness in her that seemed more powerful than the answers to his problems he had come up with hitherto. The promise she represented rivalled what he felt about his shady external demeanour and his inner turmoil.

The ball was in his court, he supposed, and he began to walk in her direction. Kate was soon introducing him to Barney the sheepdog, who had followed her home one evening when she was out walking.

Michael knelt down to stroke Barney, and his conversation with Kate resumed. This time around, she hardly mentioned God and he neatly skirted religion, faith and the metaphysical matters. What was equally unexpected was that, although complete strangers earlier that day, something seemed to have "clicked" between them. After an hour or so spent sitting on the weather-beaten bench, he began to see her as a kindred spirit. Putting his self-destructive impulses aside, Michael felt the almost physical dropping of a weight from his shoulders. Every word, revelation and disclosure left him lighter.

With God out of the picture, Michael felt compelled to explain his unhappy relationship with his father. Meanwhile, Kate divulged elements of her own past, although she seemed to prefer listening. He sensed her empathising on a deeper level than anyone else had in years, almost on a par with his mother.

Even so, talking with a stranger about his inner thoughts and depressing feelings so quickly, and in a state of sobriety, was unsettling. However, as the hours passed, dark clouds had begun to form over the loch. The time had come to stop talking, despite the benefit he was feeling. He craved his bed, and having reached it, he curled himself into a ball.

Thirty-Seven

The next day, Michael found himself craving company once more. He needn't have worried though. After a quick shave and shower, he went downstairs to find Kate chatting with his landlady inside the B&B's reception area. Kate waved and her presence roused him from his mental slumber.

It was raining heavily but she was smiling widely, which further lifted his mood. Her hair was wet and he saw she was soaked through so he led her to his room, retrieved a towel from the bathroom, and handed it to her.

"Thanks," she said, and sat on the only chair, next to the window. She watched the downpour for a moment, then turned to him. "Are we getting ahead of ourselves?"

Michael, admiring her frankness, replied, "I'm not sure," before adding, "I'm feeling a little awkward."

"About what?" she said as she dried her hair.

"Too much too soon, I suppose."

She lost her smile and said, "All the boozers down at The Friar are asking about you."

Michael was stumped for a second.

"Our local… The Black Friar," she said, smiling.

"Not anyone called Jeff, by any chance?" he asked.

She shook her head. "No, wrong gender. Someone called Sharon. She saw you stumbling your way home the other night."

Embarrassed, Michael nodded. "I thought her name was Sheila."

Kate stared at him, waiting for him to continue. After a moment's pause, she asked, "Do you have some sort of mental condition?"

Michael sighed. "I've got my problems, I suppose."

Her hair dry, Kate looked at him. "You're trying to confront your demons?"

Demons? Michael considered his reply. Demons, in the traditional sense, were for horror films and books. Real demons hid and resided within every human being he'd ever met, including his guest. Because, despite her preaching and contented demeanour, Michael was sure she'd made her fair share of wrong decisions.

"I've tried. It's called Prozac," he replied.

"Chemicals and booze aren't the answer," she said, the towel still in her hands.

Michael smiled to cover his disagreement. "You have to believe in something else too, I suppose?"

Kate nodded and, despite his reticence, they started talking once again about God and other aspects of the metaphysical. Perhaps because of his earlier epiphany about the importance of talking and sharing, he surprised himself by actually listening.

They talked for around three hours. Michael's anxiety was alleviated by having interacted with someone who seemed to give a damn about him. However, given the extreme case of panic he'd experienced in his past, he found that wasn't hard.

Perched on the edge of the bed, he found himself listening intently and feeling, in equal measures, a sense of attraction and the willingness to open himself up. The former had less to do with sexual attraction, although he again noted her figure, and was more akin to the emotion he had previously reserved only for his mother. Was it really love he now felt?

This was curious. Just a day ago, Kate had been a complete stranger. Considering his mental state during the last few months, he felt doubtful. The butterflies of sexual attraction and acceptance were fluttering within the pit of his stomach. He was becoming transfixed by what she had to say. His mood was elevated. For once, his mind was responding to a chemical reaction that was not illicit. Perhaps this was a high that wouldn't dissipate within hours into a downer.

As they talked, though he mainly listened, he found his path into rumination about his past was fading. The relief and elation he felt was eerily similar to the way he had felt after professional counselling sessions. And yet here he was, being taken back into the past, albeit the positive past following therapy.

As he listened, he began to find it a chore to separate his past from his present, and he felt a sense of elation and relief akin to how he had felt within the walls of the room in which his many counselling sessions had taken place. Drying his eyes in front of a room full of strangers. Being accepted and received into a roomful of favourable and encouraging comments. Lifted on them. Taking the support directed at him alone. Love and encouragement akin to his mother's: unconditional. A physical high different to the highs of drugs.

He would usually finish those evenings at the nearest pub, sitting on a stool at the bar, downing whisky and lager. Reflective, not down. Except the guilt and anger would return, so much so that the bartender would notice, which was when his mood would really dip. Intoxication would undo all the good work of therapy and he would fall again into that deep well of melancholy.

On his way home, he usually hailed a taxi which took him out of the town centre. The ride home seemed to take forever, trundling over potholes, bumps and ridges as they approached the deserted hills. Gazing out of the windscreen, Michael had attempted to allow the scenery to lift his spirits, although he knew coming home to his mother's loving greeting would always do the trick. His dad had deserted them a few years back now and things were a hell of a lot more peaceful. As that summer had elapsed, and as he approached his twenty-third birthday, he felt as though he had taken on his father's role, minus the bullshit attitude.

Whatever the malady, his mother's company always cheered Michael to a point bordering on the spiritual. As he sat with her loosely embracing him, sharing a bench at the rear of the house, he listened to her soothing words and let them take effect on his lingering depression. The words and their meaning took second place. Her accepting presence, hearing and feeling the rush of the river, like a chiming mobile above a child's cot: a comforting, predictable, hypnotic melody.

Back with Kate, the peaceful mood lingered.

The pair left the guest house around lunchtime and went for a meal at the local bar, moving on to small talk to avoid the heavy philosophy they'd discussed that morning. Kate, a Methodist teetotal vegetarian, nursed a lemonade. Michael drank the same, but his came with two shots of vodka. She plumped for a terrible-looking vegetable curry.

Michael wasn't a fan of curries spicier than the average korma. Even a bog standard madras saw him reaching for a glass, not of water, but silver-topped milk, which was all the better for soothing a delicate mouth and stomach. He didn't find it butch or manly, burning your tongue and the roof of your mouth. When it came to image, men could be so full of shit.

They talked at length about Kate's own struggles, strengthening his feelings for her. But by now, he had to admit his intentions towards her were becoming more amorous. Kate's coping methods had nothing to do with drink, drugs or anything of the kind he was used to. They came from faith and, although dissatisfied with God, Michael found himself almost mesmerised by her words.

A couple of hours passed but Michael craved more. He suggested a walk along the loch but Kate said she was busy, so they arranged to meet the following day. Michael headed back towards the loch and the highlands beyond it, accompanied only by a small half-drunk bottle of vodka secreted in the inside pocket of his leather jacket.

He strolled towards the hills, sat and took a long swig from the bottle. For a while, he thought of very little and was stimulated only by the burning sensation in his gullet. There wasn't enough in the bottle to get him even slightly drunk but, he found, getting plastered was not, for once, at the top of his agenda. He even mulled over why he even needed vodka when he was so buzzed by his budding relationship with Kate. Given his current state, he unexpectedly found himself reflecting on the time he'd indulged in, what he'd thought at the time, was his very last fix.

The carpet was so thin it might as well have been linoleum. A battered couch lay at the head of the room and the floor was littered with a rich variety of hazardous rubbish, including used syringes.

Unlike most of the house's patrons, Michael didn't inject heroin and had felt, from the very beginning, he had nothing in common with the rest of the crowd. For one, he didn't need to work or steal for his fix and secondly, he didn't consider himself dependent or addicted. He often told himself his drug use was purely recreational. But suddenly the prospect of losing his last fifty pound note for a further heroin high made him feel depressed so, avoiding the room's accumulated health hazards by walking around the edges, he tugged open the front door and began to venture the few miles home.

It was about six on a damp and dismal winter's morning. Over the horizon, the sun had begun to appear. He wasn't alone though. Night workers, shrugging off their twelve-hour shifts, were heading home to their beds, able to do nothing but eat and sleep before yet another gruelling shift at their four-on-four-off jobs. Michael felt like an outcast or a free spirit in their midst as he wasn't tied to a nine-to-five. Shrugging, he continued to stroll and avoided their curious gazes. He tried not to focus on the way their dusty uniforms showed him up as a well-dressed, middle-class intruder with too much money in his back pocket. He certainly didn't look like a junkie, but he definitely wasn't one of the workers either.

Michael felt at home. He'd always been, maybe always would be, an outsider. His adoring, but sick and ageing mother had become his only companion. He began to cry, wiping at his eyes so as not to be noticed. They'd given her up to six months to live and he was adamant he would kick his habits by the time she passed over. The simple truth, however, was that when he was high, his mind was able to suppress the dread and premature grief he was feeling. It helped collude with what the sober tended towards in all situations: denial.

All of these thoughts followed him home that morning. Breathing in the crisp morning air and leaving behind the enormous chimney stacks of the neighbouring industrial complex, he entered the better-off neighbourhood with which he was more familiar.

Here his social status changed. Here, he was considered as belonging to a group which was bottom-of-the-ladder, and Michael, hanging on to the bottom rung by just his fingernails, passed through this affluent part of town where bedroom curtains would remain closed for at least another hour, and where the residents held down white-collar jobs of nine-to-five drudgery. They may have viewed themselves as existing in the higher echelons, but they still worked alongside their pay packet dependent blue-collar co-workers.

Marx had been right about many things, thought Michael as he passed the Victorian-era houses lining the streets. As he pulled the door key to one of these properties from his pocket, he lit himself a cigarette.

Inside, the hall was dark and dreary. The sun had almost cleared the horizon though the light waned as the ancient oak swayed and creaked in the breeze.

Heading for the conservatory, he stubbed out his cigarette in a nearby ashtray and sat in a recliner to watch as the storm built up at a ferocious speed. Michael loved storms though and he was in his element, cocooned in the dry conservatory. He watched while rain picked up pace and collided with the recent extension as he waited for his mother to rouse from her sleep.

When the pain was less severe, she was able to sleep well and hold a coherent conversation. But, on occasions, she could focus on nothing beyond eating, sleeping and trying to calm her laboured breathing. The painkillers she'd been prescribed didn't help, and she would often become confused and light-headed, struggling even to string her words together. And yet the pills she was on right now were rocket fuel. Michael had downed a couple of them once and had been spaced out for the better part of the day.

In the conservatory, he carried on daydreaming. He fought the urge to sleep and waited patiently for any sound of movement from the back bedroom on the first floor. His mother had become a late riser recently. Those early starts, between six or seven o'clock, followed by a hard graft within or without the household had become a thing of the past. Michael gave his utmost when it came to keeping the house clean and tidy, though he had sealed off several rooms that had once served as spares for visiting guests.

This thought made Michael smile ruefully: there never had been any visiting guests. Neither his mother nor himself had ever been allowed them, and yet his father had always insisted on their upkeep, nevertheless. He'd been immature, peevish and obsessive over anything related to the house and Michael and his mother had been expected to obey and uphold his stringent standards. Even during his childhood, he had not tolerated toys being left out; they had to be stacked neatly in a toy box which Michael would only receive permission to delve inside as a reward for "good behaviour", such as displaying nuggets of knowledge from the books his dad was obsessed with.

Michael hoped that news of his dying wife would not prick his father's conscience enough for him to return. If he did, how would he react? He hoped to God the bastard wouldn't come. And if he did feel guilty, Michael wouldn't be able to cope with that either. That would lead him to ask for forgiveness, which Michael had neither the inclination nor the capacity to give.

The sound of movement, followed by the flushing of a toilet, came to him as Michael tried his best to keep his eyes open. He was done with thinking for the moment and so left the conservatory and headed back through the main hall to the kitchen near the bottom of the stairs. He shuffled over to the ceramic-topped island at the centre of the room, filled up the kettle and plugged it in. His mother always insisted on strong tea as soon as she awoke. This helped her to wake up and prepare her for the day ahead. Not even cancer could disrupt the ritual, nor the casual conversation she attempted between sips of her brew.

But this morning was different. Michael had been told by the doctors that the cancer would spread throughout her body and into her brain, and proof of the development was about to be made evident. His mother struggled down the stairs to the kitchen and she nursed the tea Michael served, but suddenly the mug up-ended and smashed onto the kitchen's cold stone floor, spilling the scolding hot liquid onto her dressing gown. Michael had been resisting pleas from the doctor to have his mother admitted into hospital, but now he realised there was nothing more he could do for her but pray for a quick and painless death. After the ambulance arrived, and his mother had laid her eyes upon her home for the final time, Michael sobbed uncontrollably all the way to the hospital.

Once there, she began to slip in and out of consciousness and Michael realised her time wouldn't be long. Indeed, a shorter ending would be a blessing all round. The release of death comes to all. Rich, poor, old, young, lost or saved, all face equally the absolute certainty of the end of conscious thought. Even so, Michael was overcome with rage. He had witnessed his mother's deterioration in a sterile, soulless hospital bed and was now at the start of his own painful journey into grief and denial. He found himself wishing for the comforting thoughts of an all-encompassing God, replete with an entourage of well-meaning, benevolent angels, waiting patiently for his mother's arrival.

Sitting there and feeling lost, he watched on helplessly as his mother lost consciousness for the last time and, while he held her hand a little too tightly, he began to weep as the monitor recording her heartbeats abruptly flat-lined.

A doctor rushed into the cubicle, but, despite his years of education and training, was completely impotent. Her fate had been passed over to a God which she had always devoutly believed in; a kind and benevolent entity which now had chosen to rip her away from the world and, more importantly, away from him.

Since then, Michael had found it a challenge to open his heart to any other woman. His connection with Kate was the first he'd experienced with any member of the opposite sex in more than ten years. It was as though the death of his mother had displaced those feelings in him. As though to feel them again would be to dishonour her memory or perhaps it was she alone who had held the monopoly on supporting him emotionally.

Over an hour after Kate's departure, Michael watched as the sun set. Although he had spent decades wrapped in interleaving states of past and present, now, for the first time, he felt curious about the future. Maybe he was kidding himself. After all, he'd only known her a day or so. And yet this was the first time, in all those years, where he had the motivation to look beyond just lust.

Hedonism had taken him so far. Those were the moments when he had managed to live in the present. But now his thoughts turned to the passing kindness of strangers. He counted Kate amongst their number. Others had touched upon his life, but whatever trace they had left, Michael had chosen to ignore. Ignorance may at times seem like bliss but being truthful to yourself was paramount. Although the vodka bottle was not yet empty, he threw it out into the choppy loch.

On the short walk home from the banks of the loch and the lapping waves, Michael accepted his mother was gone. His oath, made at St Andrews' pier, had been to die within the year. Now he made a new one: to accept the kindness of passing strangers.